ISBN 978-1-331-44878-5
PIBN 10191617

THE SOROSIS

XVI. NOVEMBER, 1909 No. 1

SHAKESPEARE ON UNIVERAL SUFFRAGE.

kespeare is not a doctrinist. an artist. It is dangerous to philosophic, religious, or polititudes into his dramas. The · who does so is apt to end nding support both for and st his theory, like the Devil's power over the quoted Scrip- Now and then, however, er consciously or unconsciousnakespeare does speak out in takable terms. Even then the is in no wise to be lost sight of Preacher. His Doctrine comes, to say, as an inference rather as a homily. Let us briefly o one instance of Shakespeare, octrinist.

commonly think of him as the st dissector of individual charthe World's Literature has ced. He has given us an array ple—studied from within and without—such as no other poet ndertaken. But he was more hat. He was the psychologist bs as well. And it is in his of mob moods and mob pashat we get—by inference only nevertheless unmistakably — what I like to call his doctrine of limited suffrage, although it is probable that he had never heard either the term used or the doctrine expounded. His interest in it is awakened first at the close of his second period. It broadened and deepened with his experience of life throughout his bitter third period. And it was in the end the last element of bitterness to yield to the forebearance and sweetness of his fourth period.

As we shall describe the element, it is to be found in three plays coming from the three last periods of his productivity. It is seen first in the Henry IV plays of 1598. It is enlarged in the Julius Caesar of 1601. It becomes the central theme and the complete philosophy of the Cariolanus of 1609. Thus its beginning falls at the height of his brilliant second period when Folstaffian chronicles and Forest of Arden Comedies popularized and sweetened his fame. Its development falls at the opening of his long line of great tragedies in which the frailties and failures of man's way with man and the harshness of blind fate's sway over men make the period one of irony, bitterness, and disbelief. Its culmination falls just at the passing of Shakespeare's soul from the turbulent unfaith of the great third period to the serene and deep-builded faith of his last romances.

In these three plays, then, is to be found a progressive but a consistent treatment of the doctrine of popular sovereignty. Moreover it is an arraignment of democracy, fiercer, bitterer than either Ibsen's in a Pillar of Society or Scott's in The Lady of the Lake. It best finds expression in Coriolanus Act III, Scene 1, Verse 40, where he says the commonalty are "such as cannot rule, nor ever will be ruled." He impeaches the uncurbed passions of the multitude, their license, their blindness to demagoguery and deeping, their fickleness and instability, their sensitive self pride and purchaseableness, their ingratitude, in short all the base qualities that attach to the ravenous and stampeding herd.

Shakespeare gives us his first study of the theme in connection with the character of Bolingbroke who made himself King Henry IV in Richard II's stead. In an admirable speech in Act II, Scene II, of Part I, King Henry IV tells his son, Prince Hal, by what deftness and hoodwinking he won the popular multitude to his cause. The charge is lightly drawn here but neve less two charges stand out dist ly. The populace are vain and b

The arraignment increases severity however, in Part II, A Scene III. The Archbishop has advising with Lords Hastings, M bray and Bardolph, as to whe the rebels' musters are sufficier meet the King's army. The A bishop concludes with a mu which is worth quoting entire.

"The commonwealth is sick of
own choice;
Their overgreedy love hath
feited:
A habitation giddy and unsure
Hath he that buildeth on the vu
heart.—
O thou fond many! with what
applause
Didst thou beat heaven with b
ing Bolingbroke,
Before he was what thou wo
have him be!
And being now trimm'd in
own desires,
Thou, beastly feeder, art so fu
him,
That thou provok'st thyself to
him up.
So, so, thou common dog, didst
disgorge
Thy glutton bosom of the
Richard;
And now thou wouldst eat thy
vomit up,
And howl'st to find it. What
is in these times?

stage, its vanity, its blindness, its madness. It becomes indeed the big scene of the play, one of the very great scenes in all Shakespeare, the justly famous Forum scene where Brutus and Antony in turn mould the passions of the multitude over the dead body of Caesar.

Now this is significant in many ways. To begin with it is the finest, the most impressive face to face study of a mob at the point of its passions that we have anywhere in the whole range of literature. Furthermore it comes as the very climax and turning point in the play. It is absolutely necessary to the plot. It is with this scene that the resolution of the plot begins. The fickleness of the mob becomes the key to the denouncement of plot and play. Brief as the mob scene is, it could not be omitted. Shakespeare has lifted his theme into vital, dramatic action, has changed it from its former descriptive subordination to a treatment swift and powerful and deep enough to reveal the stages in the mob's mad mood.

All this of course might have been done for art's sake alone. That is true. But look a little farther. Tucked away in the same act is a short scene, wholly unnecessary to the plot or to the picture. Shakespeare crowds in a short page additional to reveal the extent of the mob madness. I refer to the scene in which the mob kills the poet Cinna merely because his name is the same as that of the conspirator Cinna. The dramatist swept on in his mob study to the mad end of the picture. He wishes us to see it all—fickleness, passionateness, folly.

In Coriolanus the theme becomes even more prominent. It is no longer packed into the turning point of the plot; it is expanded until it becomes the whole plot. The mob is the plot, the main theme, the philosophy, the atmosphere, the complete play. Just when Shakespeare's treatment of madness, of fate's undiscriminating injustice, of man's brutality, of woman's baseness, of evil's dominance in the affairs of men, is softening, is sinking, is preparing to yield to the idyllic beauty and peace of the Winter's Tale and the Tempest, he recovers his bitter irony long enough to give this fiercest of all his judgments of the "beastly commoners," of the "mutable and rank-scented many."

In Coriolanus then his arraignment is the fiercest. It is also the most detailed, the longest, and the most condemnatory and convincing. It appears and reappears throughout the play. Moreover, it is not merely a study of the passionate mob as in Julius Ceasar. There Antony found the people stirred to their depths by the incidents of the day—the offering of the crown to Caesar, the excitement of the games, and the murder of Caesar. Antony himsel armed with Caesar's will. E thing joined to bring the mob t brink of hysterics. We see fickle and mad under intense porary emotion.

Not so in Coriolanus. Ther fickleness is traced backward forward, receding, advancing, sionate, deliberate, though the weeks consumed by the plot a The herd have had time to coo to ponder, to deliberate and t cide. Their choice is not passi and does not need to be blind. have wise and good men to fc Still they are fickle and foolish. they are dupes of the demago Sicinius and Brutus, men who sessed no part of the greatne Antony nor of the power of a sar's will. The fawning of bas and the appeal to the commc avarice are sufficient even placed over against the nobili Coriolanus and the welfare of city. Head and heart are false. common heard are not to be tr As Ibsen says, "the majority a ways wrong." Universal su fails. It is then and remain most perfect justification o righteousness and wisdom of tocracy where Democracy r only passionate fickleness and folly.

This, let me repeat, is an art s Shakespeare is artist, not propa

But one wonders, in the light ɜse three plays, what he would ɔday about universal suffrage if he could study bossism and suffragetism.

George W. Putnam.

"MARY WILKINS AS A SHORT STORY WRITER."

ɜry new writer of short stories, ıs the age of their highest dement, presents his or her ideas in some new and attractive Mary Wilkins' stories are individual in tone. Perhaps no writer could have presented imple themes in quite such an ɜsting style. Her stories, al;h not very unusual, are simple, to life, and reflect a peaceful, atmosphere.

I read her stories through, they ıo very deep impression upon ıs to their substance. The ht did not seem to me very un- nor especially strong. They n no very strong character dement, although some might that they were written chiefly ıe character portrayal. Her ters are almost all women, and ent only a few types. Parhaps omen are quiet, gentle, and tempered; perhaps they are tive, but finally repentant. At te they are all very simple and asily understood.

her are the themes she sets ıew or very deep. They main- ur interest principally by the r in which they are disclosed. are simple, everyday themes. They teach simple, everyday lessons. Perhaps it is the simplicity of the stories more than anything else that appeals to us. Her tone suits her subject in everyway. Herein her stories are artistic. Her sentences are simple in construction, for the most part short, and the tone seems very abrupt and swift. She chooses simple, ordinary words, too. Although we feel a sympathetic undertone throughout, although we feel that she is always deeply interested in the subject she is treating, yet one might almost call the general tone cold,—at any rate we might call the tone,—New England.

Mary Wilkins' stories are all true to life. They tell of everyday fact, of circumstances and conditions that might surround people at any time. She portrays homely life entirely. She pictures to us the lower classes, and the things that happen to them, the questions that come to them.

We always feel that they are possible. The habit of living alone, which had become a necessity to the gray little New England nun seems very real to us. The suffering of Hannah, who sacrificed her life to save the good name of the man she loved awakens our pity and admiration, and our joy for her in the end. The great disappointment and disillusionment that hastened the death of the poor little poetess, and crushed her to the earth, makes us feel a great sympathy for her. Such things as these may come unto the lives of any of us, especially of those surrounded on all sides by poverty.

Mary Wilkins' stories are to me, however, principally atmosphere stories. This seems to me to be their most admirable characterist They breathe a very sweet atn phere. We feel it at once, and under the spell of it immediat They breathe peacefulness, and r and quiet. They make one thinl flowers and of delicate beauty. S you want to take them for their cl acters or themes, do so; but they not be so pleasing. Rather take tl for their atmosphere of peace.

Elvira Estep, '1

SKETCHES

THE FIELD.

Do you remember the field behind the pines on Sunset Hill? How glorious it was that last Sunday when late in the afternoon we climbed up to escape the guests and the polite conversation! The sky was blue with white fleecy clouds in it, and the field, dotted with clusters of daisies, glimmered in the light of the setting sun. As we lay under the pines and looked down past the hedge of bushes and trees at the bottom, and on over the other bright green fields, the whole place seemed happy and living.

We saw the field again at night. The green had turned to silver beneath the dew and it was cold as we slushed through it. We could only see the daisies right at our feet, and as we walked along they popped out at us white and glittering. Far above was the great dark sky with thousands of shining stars in it. was as happy as before, but the s and the silence showed us a de meaning, and we went home hus with the wonder of it.

Mary D. Lindsa

If I should paint a clump of sun
trees,
All glowing crimson—one w
mass of fire,—
And, in the midst, a single m
tree,
All shining gold and yellow i
tire,
And, 'neath the whole, a weal
asters wild,
A brilliant, purple sea;—the v
would say,
"What folly! Nature never
such hues."
And yet, I saw just such a
today.

HER FIRST DAY AT SCHOOL.

:ty," she was always called by ›ody. She had never played with other children, preferring lls' society, because she could hem as she pleased, and scold at her pleasure;—or she felt little chills running down her when she started for the first o the Chester Avenue School. as a chubby little thing with curly hair, and big serious eyes, that looked frightened she found the bell had just She went solemnly in, and acher, whom she had met the efore, motioned her to a seat; she sat as near the edge as uld get without tumbling off. rst business of the day was ll, and when Miss Murray out, "Elizabeth Antionette rdson," she twisted about for ief, never-to-be-forgotten sec-o see who should answer to awful long name, — then d, twisted her dress around nger, and stammered, "Pres-She had a wild desire to rush the room, as she felt the curi-oks of the little girls, and the ssed giggle of that little boy. the aisle. She thought hotly at her father had said—that Thomas was a naughty boy she was sure now that she with him, though she had ther doubtful about it last

Spelling was the first lesson of the day, and it fell to Betty's lot to spell "rat." Well, she could do that all right, for she remembered very distinctly the letters printed beneath the picture of one in her book that Aunt Helen had given her for Christmas. It was right at the top of the 27th page, and she could see it plainly with her eyes shut. So she got up and courageously spelled "M-O-U-S-E." The bright pupils laughed, and even some that weren't very bright, and the rest of the children, as well as Bettey, wondered what everyone thought was so funny. For the rest of the morning they copied letters and numbers on their slates, and Betty was the first to proudly carry her slate up to Miss Murray, who glanced at the wierd and wonderfully made signs on it, and told her to rub them off and try again, which Betty sorrowfully but patiently did. Then lunch time came, which everyone enjoyed, but by half past two Betty was sound asleep, having missed her usual afternoon nap. Miss Murray wakened her when it was time to go, and Betty trudged wearily but joyfully homeward. That evening she said to her father, "Papa, I don't like that school. They all laughed because I couldn't tell a rat from a mouse, and," she added sleepily, "I do think you were right about Harry Thomas."

Alice Stoeltzing, '13.

A TONIC.

When your body's weak and weary
And your spirit's fagged and dreary,
Take a walk.
When you're sick and tired of lessons
And can't think of any blessin's,
Take a walk.

If you're anxious to grow fatter
Or grow thin—it doesn't matter,
Take a walk.
If you're stature you would heigl
Or your step you wish to lighte
Take a walk.

When you're in a mood for tal
And you think your friends "knocking,"
Take a walk.
If your ailments all are chronic,
You will find an "all-round toni
In a walk.

Florence K. Wilson, '

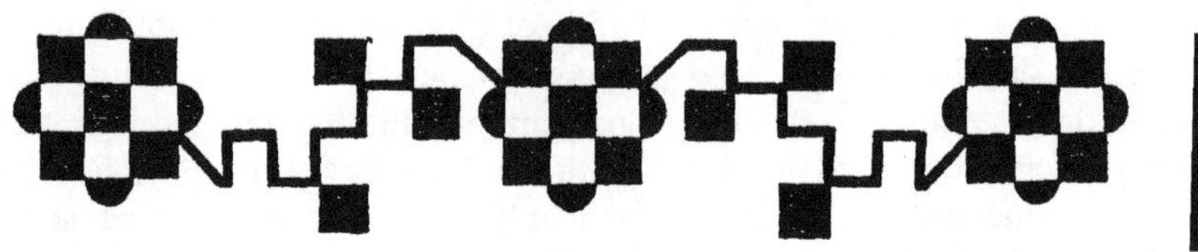

ORIAL.

short story is one of the most important and attractive items of interest in our paper, and in former years we have had reason to be proud of this department. We do not wish to fall back in any respect and would therefore encourage the "budding authors" among us to record their inspirations and let them be a benefit to their fellow beings.

A box has been placed in the library to receive contributions from the students to the "Sorosis." All stories, verses and sketches will be gladly received, subject to the approval of the Board of Editors. Requests have come in from several quarters that more attention be paid to personals and class incidents or jokes. We have no objections to receiving these items if the members of the classes will make note of them and either give them to their class representative on the "Board," or deposit them in the box in the library. The "Sorosis" is glad to take every opportunity of being the means of expressing real school spirit.

Short Story Contest!!!

The "Sorosis" announces short story contest, open to College students. A prize $5.00 will be awarded for t best story handed to the E tors before January 10, 19 Manuscripts must be writt on one side only.

ALUMNAE.

The Decade Club, II, held its first meeting of this year at the home of Miss Hilda Sadler, on Friday, October 18th. Plans for the winter's work were discussed, officers were elected, and committees appointed. The officers for the coming year are:—

President—Miss Jennie McSherry.

Vice President—Miss Edna McKee.

Secretary—Mrs. Verne Shear.

Treasurer—Miss Bessie Johnson.

A Bridge Matinee was given in the ball room of the Hotel Schenley on Tuesday, October 5th, for the benefit of the Alumnae Dormitory Furnishing Fund. Miss McConnell, President of the Alumnae Association, acted as chairman of the affair and many ladies outside of the college served on her committee and gave excellent help. Thanks are due to those who helped in any way; especially to Kaufmann Brot for their gift of seven hundred cards in the College colors and the College monogram, and to following friends, for the prizes gave:—

Gillespie's Art Store, Wunde the Art Shop, Reymer's, Rob Grogan's, Reizenstein's, and H ton and Clark's.

Over two hundred guests present and, although not ma the Alumnae attended, many o guests were recognized as girls had at one time attended the lege.

The usual letter has been sen by the Lecture Committee a each member of the Alumnae ciation for her annual gift to Lecture Fund. Enough mon desired to give at least one lecture this winter.

the Alumnae meeting, October it was decided to have an ınae procession at the next mencement. This will be a ous opportunity for the Alum- o get back to the College life pirit. It is hoped that as many ie girls as possible will enter this to make it one of the most essive parts of the Commence- exercises.

s. E. Brown Baker, '13, of nectady, is visiting her parents, ınd Mrs. Philip Pfeil, of Shady ie. She came home to attend vedding of her sister Florence.

s. John Coleman, '03, of New ord, Ohio, is making her first to her parents since her mar- , which took place in the early of the summer.

s. John M. Phillips, '03, has an- little girl, Mary Templeton, in the early part of September.

s. Boyd (nee Edith Allison) n Pittsburg this fall and sang e Allegheny County Teachers' ute.

eral of the '09 girls are teach- ıis year. Miss Grace Tatnal is at Bartholomew-Clifton School, Cincinnati; Miss Emma Coulter is in Greenville, Mississippi, and Miss Leila Estep is in Aliquippa.

Among the Alumnae studying at different colleges and universities are: Miss Gladwin Coburn, Miss Cohen, and Miss Irma Beard, all of '09, at Pennsylvania College for Women; Miss Lilla Greene, '08, at Columbia University; and Miss Nancy Blair, '04, at the Kindergarten College.

Miss Rebecca Eggers, '04, and Miss Anna Hunter, '03, have accepted positions in the Pittsburg High School.

Miss Mary Blair, '02, returned to Pittsburg in June, after a seven-years' sojourn in Colorado. She is at present in the Tuberculosis League Hospital, and is steadily improving in health.

Class of '02 reports another baby, Donald Littell Glass, son of Mr. and Mrs. John Glass.

Miss Edna McKee, Miss Cohen, Miss Estep, Miss Coburn, and Miss Jarecki have attended several of the social events this year.

SOUTH HALL.

several years we have been ıg forward to the time when ollege should possess a dormitory of its own, separated from that of Dilworth Hall. At last our dream is realized. Marion Crawford has said that a man's dream of Venice is the only case where the dream itself is surpassed by the reality. We can forgive Marion Crawford because he evidently had not seen South Hall. It is certainly a case where the realization has fully satisfied our wildest expectations.

There are two especially attractive features about South Hall: its situation and home-like atmosphere. But, indeed, there are so many charming characteristics that it is difficult to single out only two. The situation could not have been chosen better. Perched on the side of the hill it looks down upon a grassy, wooded amphitheater at the foot of the hill, Woodland Road, lined with maples, and the trees, homes and hills beyond, while away to the left lies a glimpse of the city hazily blue in the distance. This hill presents the most beautiful view in Pittsburg. Then South Hall is conveniently near the recitation halls, a source of thanksgiving to both students and faculty alike. The latter have been deeply impressed this term by the paucity of tardinesses, especially among the house girls.

The most striking feature of the new dormitory is the air of completeness about its furnishings, which produces an atmosphere of comfort and hominess. In the lower hall the wide-open fire-place, with its cozy ingle-nooks and roomy cushioned divan, is inviting. Beyond lies a broad veranda, amply fitte with deep swings and comfor rockers. On either side of th ception hall are two reception ro one of which is artistically hur brown and the other in our ow C. W. violet. At the southern of the building is a large, lighted dining-room. On the dc tory floors the corridors are and well lighted; the rooms and beautifully furnished in b mission vals. For the furnishir South Hall we are indebted tc labor and thoughtfulness of loyal Alumnae.

Universal delight in the bui was shown by the guests at th given by the College upon the fc opening on November 11th and and the pleasure of the studer shown every day in the nu who express their desire to l next year.

Judging by the rate of increa the student body during the year, the time must soon come P. C. W. will possess a Lindsay as well as South Hall, anc campus will be dotted not only violets, but with dormitories. they all be as attractive as Hall.

COLLEGE NOTES.

Juniors held a dance on Fri- vening, October 8th, in honor Freshmen. One of the spe- atures of the evening was a on lead by the Junior girls, and vors were very original. The g was especially pleasant, be- it was our first opportunity for ig the new girls in a social

Friday evening, October 15th, Coolidge gave her annual din- r the College girls and faculty. s were laid for a hundred and -two guests. Doctor Lindsay short talk and the Freshmen velcomed by the other classes, Tassey speaking for the s, Miss Diescher for the s, and Miss Bickel for the mores. Miss Blair responded e Freshmen. After dinner ody sang the College songs, y the Glee Club, then went South Hall and danced the the evening.

ay evening, October 1st, the Girls" entertained the "New with an informal dance in As- Hall. A good time generally ident, in spite of the fact that seemed to have an especial for the floor. Refreshments, ing of ice cream, cake and , were served.

Over a hundred guests were present at the dance given by the Sophomores for the students and faculty on Friday evening, October 22nd. There was a cotillion led by the Sophomores, with yellow roses for favors, and a moonlight waltz. Several of the Alumnae were present.

Mr. Whitmer has taken charge of the chapel services, and is making several changes in the form of service; special features are reserved for Wednesday morning. A choir, composed of girls of the College Glee Club, has been organized to lead the singing, and after the devotional services Mme. Graziani and several of the girls have sung, and Mr. Whitmer and Miss Crowe have played on the organ. The services are very much more effective and interesting.

Doctor Lindsay is delivering a series of fifteen talks after the devotional services on Wednesday mornings. He has taken up such subjects as "What is Philosophy?" "What is Idealism?"

The Dramatic Club has discussed plans for the work this year, and the different classes have decided upon the plays and entertainments they will present. An open meeting of the Club was held on Monday afternoon, November 8th. Miss Kerst gave several readings and light refreshments were served afterwards. The Club wants a large and enthusiastic membership this year, for the work is going to be very interesting. The new officers are:—

President—Miss Crowe.
Vice President—Miss Kramer.
Secretary—Miss Florence Wilson.
Treasurer—Miss Hickson.
Business Manager—Miss Bic

The Athletic Association ha organized for this year, with th lowing officers:—

President—Miss Lindsay.
Secretary and Treasurer — Bickel.

COLLEGE CLASSES.

The officers of the Senior Class are:—

President—Miss McKibbin.
Vice President—Miss Kramer.
Secretary and Treasurer — Miss Tassey.

The Junior officers are:—
President—Miss Diescher.

The new Sophomores officers are:—

President—Miss Bickel.
Vice President—Miss Hardy.
Secretary—Miss Estep.
Treasurer—Miss Davis.

Freshman officers:—
President—Miss Blair.
Vice President—Miss Young.
Secretary—Miss Kingsbacher.
Treasurer—Miss Shutt.

Dr. Christie, of the Theological Seminary in Allegheny, gave the following lecture on "Burns," before the Faculty and College Students Wednesday evening, Novembe

Robert Burns was born o 25th of January, 1759, at a smal tage in the parish of Alloway, two miles southwest of the to Ayr. The poet's father was occ as a gardener upon the estat gentleman until 1776, when h Alloway and leased a farm nea The father was a man of su understanding, and of the s upright, self-respecting charac honorably distinctive of the Scotch peasantry, and all the of his married life seemed to been a constant struggle to tain a decent living and to e his family. At an early age I and his brother were sent to at Alloway, about a mile from To these means of educatio added the few books in the f possession; among which wa lect collection of English son these songs, Burns says, "I over them, driving my cart o ing to labor, song by song, ve carefully noting the true r or sublime, from affectation ıstion. I am convinced that I to this practice much of my craft, such as it is."

: Ayrshire farm proved an unssful undertaking; and the fammoved to another farm only to with like misfortune, culminat- financial ruin, which was fol- almost immediately by the of the father. During these of poverty, Burns grew to ood. In his sixteenth year, in- by his first love "for a bonny, sonsie lass," his companion in arvest field, he composed his verses to accompany an air she was wont to sing.

er their father's death, Robert ilbert Burns took a farm. But ilure of their crops discouraged Some of his poems handed in manuscript among his asso- gained him reputation—but l the unfavorable attention of irk Session toward him. He nade preparations to emigrate ıaica and to assist in raising for his passage he published ems, and was then able to se- steerage passage on a vessel to sail. He had taken leave friends and had composed his ll to "Old Coila's hills"—when from Dr. Blacklock, who had is poems and recognized his , changed his plans and sent) Edinburgh to be suddenly ted into the society of men of the highest distinction, who received him as one of themselves. He was then enabled to gratify his desire of visiting some of the most beautiful spots of Scotland and England. He made several tours, returning in the intervals to Edinburgh, where caressed and feted on all sides, he formed those habits of dissipation, which led to wrecked health and an early death.

In 1788 Burns left Edinburgh. He purchased a little farm of Ellisland, near Dumfries, made a public declaration of marriage with Jean Armour and took up his residence on the farm. To his calling of farmer he united that of exciseman, having been appointed a post which paid him at first £50 a year. His farm was too often neglected. He was welcome in the best society of the neighborhood and occupied himself in composing songs for a musical work. Later he removed to Dumfries. Here the habit of intoxication grew upon him. Yet it gives one a thrill almost to think of this great poet, oppressed with the cares of a family, drudging through a hard, uncongenial and most scantily paid employment, the fineness of his nature dimmed by drink, his strong frame beginning to feel the inroads of disease, yet rising superior to all low-hearted suggestions, and with a glorious burst of patriotic love, refusing to be a penny the richer in pocket for the pure ore of everlasting song with which he again and again dowered his country.

So day by day—the shadows darkened—ill health, mental dejection and pecuniary straits had now encompassed Burns on every side. His last few years were very sad and hard ones, but he died honorably and no blemish darkens his name—which one of us is pure or worthy enough to disapprove. It is true that Burns lived a life which was far from morally pure, and contained many dark incidents which we would do well to forget; but let us deal mercifully in our censuring of the man, recalling the period in which he lived, those with whom he asso(and the customs and practices o day. And let us remember him as the man whose talent Scc loves to honor, and whose sc song and music finds a tender in the heart shrine of every lan people today.

For his poetry is of the peopl for the people, its tender senti its wonderful depth of insigh feeling has erected for the ploughman a monument, gr and purer and loftier than the of man could ever build.

Fancesca Alden Cameron,

PERSONALS.

Mr. Roger Greene, who is attending Marietta College, visited his sister, Margaret, Saturday, October 9th.

Mr. and Mrs. A. E. Young, of Vandergrift, Pa., spent the day with their daughter, Martha, at South Hall, Saturday, October 2nd.

Mr. Grant Spiher, of Vandergrift, Pa., paid a short visit to his sister Freda, Friday, October 8th.

Mrs. K. G. Shutt, of Warren, Pa., while on a visit to Pittsburg friends, spent a short time with her daughter, Maude, of South Hall, during the first week in October.

Back "in the dim dead day yond recall," it was once su and we all had a vacation ar faculty had one too. Part of it abroad and part of it, like the of us, found rest and enjoymen at home. All of it, howeve natural it may seem, enjoyed it period of freedom from us.

Miss Coolidge spent several on the Maine Coast. The rest summer was passed at her h Fitchburg, Mass.

Last year's Seniors had Kerst as their guest at their party, held at Rye Beach, or Erie. We infer that "As Yo as the only rule of the party. Kerst afterwards took a trip on ıkes.

s Green enjoyed her vacation home in Ohio.

. Armstrong "rusticated," so id, at her home in Vandergrift,

Martin spent part of the sum- ı a hunting trip in behalf of the e. The game sought for was -his ammunition, praise of our ıs Alma Mater. Has anyone d that the Freshman Class is ally large this year?

ɔpe was favored with visits ɔur representatives of our Col- his summer. Germany and each claimed two.

Skilton attended lectures at niversity of Leipzig for five and then spent the rest of the r in traveling through Ger- and Switzerland. Two weeks assed in Switzerland and then urn home was made by way Rhine, Holland and England.

ish is again being taught at stand by Mr. Putnam, who een in Germany since last ry. While abroad he was as- professor in English in the iche Gymnasium at Kolberg on the Baltic. Mr. Putnam was appointed to this position by the Carnegie Foundation for the Advancement of Teaching under the exchange arrangement with Prussia.

Madame de Vallay's vacation was spent in Paris. She went there by way of Gibralter, Morocco, and Spain. A few weeks were also spent in London and in Stratford-on-Avon.

We were all very much interested in hearing Miss Brownson tell of her experiences in Geneva, and we would like to present her with some time to tell us about the rest of her trip. She visited Holland, studied several weeks in Paris, and took a short trip through the Chateau country in France.

Miss Dulany is very tenderhearted. She weeps when she looks at a little dead worm, and Biology is out of the question.

The Sophomores think that the dreams of the rarebit fiend aren't even to be compared with the pictures we draw in Biology Class.

Miss Carla Jarecki visited at the College for two weeks this fall.

Did you ever see a Freshman when she hadn't just written a theme, was going to write one, or was looking for an inspiration?

Miss Blair (Freshman)—I don't care for Lamb's essays,—I prefer Bacon.

Miss Hogue—"That reminds me."

Mr. Martin, proving a geometrical proposition just before the Hallowe'en party:

Hypothesis—I will be there as Mephistopheles.

To prove—That I will make the hit of the evening.

Proof.—(?)

A Junior upon being asked to write a poem, submitted the following:—

"See the little birdies
A standing on their legs;
'Twas not so many months a
That they were only eggs.'

A "bold, bad Sophomore" is g of telling the following joke, v she claims is original: "A Swe a gymnasium went up a Pole; a top the Swede took French l came down the Pole (pole) a sian (a-rushing), and danced German at the foot, with a fe his friends congregated there." question was asked the auth this pun, "Didn't the knee (Negro) as the Swede came the Pole a Russian?" but the a was not willing to commit hers

Y. W. C. A.

President—Maude Demmler.
Vice President—Ethel Tassey.
Secretary—Margaret Connelly.
Treasurer—Grace Dulany.

The Y. W. C. A. held a reception for the men students Friday evening, September 24th. Instead of dances, the program contained lists of musical numbers which were filled out as conversational engagements. Miss Drais and Miss Crandall furnished the music in their usual pleasing style. There were several guessing contests. Miss Margaret Bensall received the first prize in guessing advertisements; Miss Margaret Patton gettin "booby." Miss Sarah Stuck took the first prize for word ing and Miss Vivian Stitt wa soled with the "booby." Towa close of the evening a dainty was served.

The regular Y. W. C. A. m of Tuesday, September 28th given over to the delegates to tain Lake Park, whose report a graphic account of the proce of the Student Convention there last June. Every year o sociation sends representati this great convention. They ɔe impressed by the inspira- l incentive given to this work by such a gathering of students from the different colleges.

MUSIC NOTES.

Glee Club has been reorgan- d is in charge of Madame i. The membership has been ed to about thirty-five. The going to try to make this successful year. The new are:

dent—Miss Crowe.

tary and Treasurer—Miss

. Graziani gave a delightful ecital in the Chapel on Tues- ovember 9th. She also sang pening of South Hall, on Fri- d Saturday, November 12th h, Miss Leedom accompany-

y morning, November 12th, composed of Miss Stephens, all and Miss Donovan gave ein's "The Angel." Miss Kerr, pupil of Mme. Graziani, ng a charming little Rus- ghtingale song.

Orchestral Concerts have be- d have been well attended by lege girls.

Mabel Crowe, pupil of Mr. er, played two organ selec- t the Chapel Wednesday g—Cradle song, and Scher- y Rheinberger.

Miss Harrington gave her second short recital in the Chapel on the morning of November 16th. Her program was as follows:

Er ist Gekomnen.............Franz
Du bist die Ruh'..........Schubert
Unmindful of the Roses...Schneider
Bird Raptures ....Schneider
Vagabondia ....Harrington

On Friday evening, November 19th, Mr. Whitmer will give a lecture recital on Debussy's opera of "Pelleas and Melisande," Miss Kerst reading the last two acts to the rarely beautiful music of this opera. Extremely typical of modern French writing, Debussy's opera is one of vital interest to musicians. It is epoch making. A thoroughly enjoyable evening is anticipated.

Madame Graziani, contralto, and Mr. Luigi von Kunits, violinist, will give a recital December 3rd. The program is most attractive. This is Mme. Graziani's Pittsburg debut, and is eagerly looked forward to. Mr. von Kunits is an artist of high standing and is well known.

An interesting feature of chapel services, recently introduced, is the original organ responses, written by the music students of the College.

Wednesday morning has been chosen for special chapel services. A long program, consisting regularly of: The Prelude, Invocation, Chant, several Hymns and Postlude, with occasional soloists and an ac has been arranged. This servi ing "special," attracts visitors College on that day, and Wedr might well be called "Vistor's

OMEGA NOTES.

October twenty-first, the society held its first annual meeting in the reception room. The subject chosen for the year is: first semester, American novelists of today, and, second semester, modern English novelists. The first author considered was Gen. Lew Wallace and his novel, "Ben Hur." The programme as follows:

Paper...........Sara Carpenter, '11
"Life of Lew Wallace."

Paper............Mary Kramer, '10
"Ben Hur."

Sketch............Mabel Crowe, '11

At a meeting held November the eleventh, the programme co of "The Life of S. Weir Mitch Sara Carpenter, '11, "Hugh W by Rosalie Supplee, '11, and Other Works of S. Weir Mit by Irma Diescher, '11.

November eighteenth the ing new members were initiat the society:

Maggie May McCullongle,
Margaret Greene, '11.
May Hardy, '12.
Eleanore Davis, '12.
Beulah Pierce, '12.

EXCHANGES.

following exchanges have eceived: "The Washington-onian," "The Muhlenberg," chool Journal," "The Juniata "The Buchtelite," "The a," "The Agnetian Monthly," Holcad," "The Crimson and "The Olio."

"Washington - Jeffersonian" s an article, "An Ex-College Advice to His Kid Brother," ought to be noted by Fresh- They also have copied an from the "Pittsburgh Post" f Rules for Students," which to us in connection with our stem of Student Government.

Laugh it Off.

ı wanted in a fight?
.augh it off.
ı cheated of your right?
.augh it off.
ıake tragedy of trifles;
hoot butterflies with rifles.
.augh it off.

our work get into kinks?
.augh it off.
ı near all sorts of brinks?
.augh it off.
ınity you're after,
no recipe like laughter—
.augh it off.

—Ex.

"Bess"

That was really her name, although I usually called her "Toodles" and it was plain to be seen we were in love with each other. She was rather shorter than the average, and to me the most beautiful being I had ever seen. She had a wealth of dark brown hair and big brown eyes radiant with love and devotion, and a smiling mouth that disclosed two perfect rows of pure white teeth. When she sat on my lap she would look up at me with those "soulful eyes," and if my face was within reach would imprint a kiss upon my cheek. Oh, the rapture of that kiss! It was like the gentle touch of an April shower—or rather like being hit in the face with a wet sponge—for she was only my bulldog, Bess.—Ex.

A lady riding in a street car in Nevada, richly attired, reading the Philistine, laid the booklet aside and removed her shoes and stockings, turned her stockings, and put them on again, and put on her shoes, paying no attention to the fellow passengers. An elderly gentleman sitting near by, very timidly said to the lady, "Pardon me, madam, allow me to ask, why this strange procedure, in the street car?

She earnestly replied, "The texts

in this booklet are so hot, I had to turn the hose on myself."

Now, to your quilting, ladies.

"Dreams."

Ah! dreams, dreams, dreams,
Ye are the heart of me!
The white ships melt in the mist-
land,
At the shadowy edge of the sea;
And where they go I do not know,
For what their names maye be,
Ah, dreams, dreams, dreams,
Ye are the heart of me!

Smith College Monthly.

This Ain't No Joke.

If you see a funny phrase,
That really makes you grin,
Don't waste it just upon yourself,
Cut it out and send it in.

—Ex.

"A word to the wise is sufficient."

THE SOROSIS

VOL. XVI DECEMBER, 1909 No. 2

THE CHRISTMAS PRINCESS.

By Francesca Alden Cameron, '11.

The Little Son sat curled up in the warm glow of the fire-light, his head pillowed cosily on the lap of his father's arm chair, his slender, brown little hands clasped tenderly about the Christmas gift. It was tied up daintily in white tissue paper and red ribbons—Lisette, the nurse had just finished the arrangement of the last bow, and she had left him with tears in her eyes—tears which the Little Son was too young to understand. "Bless his brave little heart," she murmured softly to herself, passing out through the library door. "His first Christmas gift—and the most precious thing he has. Dear, little lad—" she repeated tenderly over and over again, as her eyes wandered out through the open door to the little mound, out under the fragrant pines, where the child's mother lay sleeping —the little-girl mother whom the Little Son had never known. Her mind went back to that Christmas eve when the little mother had last smiled on her sleeping child—and clasped her jewelled picture about his tiny throat.

"To wear always in memory of me," she had whispered faintly, trying to smile in her old bright manner. "You can tell him for me, when he is old enough to understand, that on his first Christmas eve I gave it to him—my little, only son!"

And so she had died with his name on her lips and his tiny round head, cuddled close in the curve of her arm.

That was the Little Son's first Christmas eve and his mother's last—she was only a little girl when she left him—a little girl mother with laughing lips and wistful eyes, but as months and years gradually slipped away, she came back to him quite often in his dreams—and was not a memory, nor a fancy, but a living, beautiful woman whose presence seemed always near him.

And so the tiny lad had worn her portrait about his throat and carried her image within his heart for the five brief years of his life, and had lived and gone his way, in a world of dreams which the real world was too old to understand always yearning, yet seeking in vain, for his father's friendship and love. He had always, so far back as he could possibly remember for the past of a tiny five year old is very dim indeed, adored and reverenced his father from a respectful distance. The grave, silent man, with the handsome face and tired voice had never cared to know his little son in an intimate way. There had been one time only, when the child had lain in his father's arms. He had fallen and cut his head in a very severe manner, so that it was necessary for a number of stitches to be taken in order to close the wound. The father had held Little Son almost tenderly upon his knees while the surgeon did his work, the tiny patient uttering no word or cry. Then the father had looked down into the child's eyes and marvelled at their beauty and the wistfulness which rested there.

"His mother's eyes, he whispered almost brokenly to himself. "His mother's eyes."

But that was all. The accident had never served to draw them together in any way, and for a time the man seemed to avoid the very presence of the child, as though his little curl crowned head, and witching, love-lit face should serve but to recall the image of another face—and bring back all the memories which each day seemed harder to forget.

And so these two dwelt in the home apart. The beautiful old house with its rare pictures and beautiful furnishings, seemed to the child—a sleeping palace—waiting for its prince, the coming of whom was one of his dearest dreams.

He loved to fling himself down on the floor beneath his mother's picture, chin in hand gazing long and tenderly up into the charming face, and pretending that the Little Princess had awakened and the palace was brightened with sunshine again.

The Little Son had a small, girl playmate who lived in the house next door and to whom at times, he confided these wistful fancies and desires which filled his quaint, old-fashioned mind. She was only a girl—of course but she understood him in a remarkably bright and sensible manner. While visiting at her home the previous afternoon—a sentence of Beth's mother had lingered within his mind—"A Christmas gift is doubly dear—when one has denied himself to give it. For that is always the measure of one's love." Then suddenly looking down at the Little Son she had said in that kind manner of hers which he loved so well—"You too, Little Son, dear. Why do you not give something too to someone you love?"

She said no more, hushed, perhaps by the strange look which stole over the child's face. His lips were parted, the rich color came and went in his usually pale cheeks and his eyes shone with a happier light than had ever shone in their clear depths before.

"Dear, dear little fellow," she mused softly to herself with pitying tear-moist eyes. But the Little Son was too busy thinking to comprehend.

And that night, lying awake on his pillow after his prayers had been said, he pondered it all over within his mind and tried to imagine what he could give his father for a Christmas gift, which would please him most, and which he must love and cherish for the sake of the one who had sent it, denying himself in order to prove his love.

For a long time, the child puzzled on, wondering dimly for he was very tired now whether there was anything he possessed which would seem worthy in his father's eyes. And at length the idea came, so swiftly, so clearly, so inevitably that the Little Son realized there could be no mistake about it, and that his answer had come at last.

With a tired little cry, he flung himself passionately down against the pillows, the jewelled miniature which he always wore about his little throat, crushed tightly in his hands.

"Oh Daddy," he cried, "will you understand? Will you love the Princess as much as I do?" And with her dear name on his lips he fell asleep—wondering, perhaps—if it was always so hard to realize that Christmas meant love.

And so here it was come at last—their Christmas eve! At the sound of his father's steps, the Little Son rose hastily up from the warm rug where he had been lying and crept softly out into the front hall. The small figure, in its white suit and red tie stood exquisitely defined against the crimson hangings of the entrance way. His, brave little heart was beating very fast—and his breath came and went in such excited little flutters, that the child wondered whether his father might possibly hear it and be displeased.

But the great silent man seemed scarcely to notice the other's presence. A quick frown darkened his face—with an impulsive motion he jerked his hand away from the clinging fingers, and entered the library.

"Daddy—oh father!" cried the Little Son—hastening after him, and holding out the little gift to attract the man's attention. "It's for you, daddy—I mean father. A Christmas gift from me! Oh, take it, daddy, do take it."

The pleading eyes were very persuasive, and the man's heart might have softened—had it not been for the child's last words. They cut him to the very quick, but with a muttered cry of pain, or sadness or anger, I know not what, he flung the child away and dashed the package to the floor. The Little Son's eyes haunted him for hours afterwards, yet he had uttered neither word nor cry.

* * * * * * * * * * * * *

About midnight, a carriage pulled up under the porte cochêre—and the Little Son's father alighted. The Christmas stars were shining overhead, the air was filled with the crisp, fresh, odor of new fallen snow.

"Merry Christmas, Sir," the coachman called back as the carriage rolled on down the drive way, and the words repeated themselves again and again in the man's lonely heart, as he mounted the steps of his home.

The little gift still lay upon the floor where it had fallen—scarcely four short hours ago. The child's face haunted him, as it had done the entire evening, and with a strange, half resentful feeling of remorse and shame.

Drawing his easy chair up close to the fire—where the rosy flames shone brightly over his handsome sad face, he sat for a long while buried in thought, calling back with wistful tenderness, another Christmas eve. Out of the past came dim memories which haunted him and her face with its gold crowned head and tender eyes, came close and looked into his. He could not meet her eyes—for he knew the reproach which was written there. "Your Christmas Gift, sweetheart—a little son!"

His Christmas Gift! With hurried fingers—he undid the crimson bows and pretty tissues of the package. A scrap of paper fluttered to the floor. "Father"—so the Little Son had printed—with little cramped, painstaking fingers—"A mery Chrismus—from your litle sun. It's the Princess, daddy—I'm giving her back to you."

In a nest of pink cotton, lay his wife's miniature, upon a slender chain. It was as though the little girl wife of the past, had come back and slipped her hand in his for a brief while. The man crushed the tiny picture to his lips with passionate tenderness—but he could not speak. And so he lay for a long while in silence.

* * * * * * * * * * * * * *

It was very late when he arose. He meant to go to the Little Son, but he was not to be found in the nursery. His clothes were hanging beside the bed, but the latter was still untouched. They found him later in the evening, asleep upon the parlor floor, his head resting upon his arms and his cheeks still stained with the presence of recent tears. One small hand still clasped his tiny throat as though even in dream land he missed his mother's gift.

And from overhead, in the golden frame, his mother's face looked down upon him with wistful eyes, and the moonlight had given an elfish charm to all the delicate curves, and lines of the picture, so that she seemed indeed like some old princess of fairy tale days so quaint, so ethereally beautiful had grown the little face.

The father gathered the Little Son up tenderly in his arms, so softly that the child did not awake, but smiled as though he dreamt sweet dreams. One tiny hand still lay against his throat, and his brown curls brushed the fathers' lips, the moonlight gleamed across the room and through the silvered rays—the Christmas angels seemed to smile.

Not until his little head lay back upon the pillows, and his father's hand lay clasped in his, did the Little Son awake.

"Oh, Daddy," he cried in happy surprise. "Has my dream come true—and the Prince come back to the Princess—at last! We've waited and waited so long!"

"Yes, Little Son," the man answered with all his heart in the words. "The Prince has come back to you—and you father is with him, dear." So gathering the tired child close in his arms, he told him the story of the Prince's coming and of the happiness which lay in store for both.

"But—the princess, daddy!" cried the Little Son in the midst of the story his eyes anxiously scanning the father's face. "Will she know how happy we are, do you think, and will it make her happy, too."

"Yes, sweet heart," the man answered softly, kissing the child goodnight. "It will make her happy too!" and long after the Little Son's eyes were closed in slumber he sat beside him watching the Christmas stars and awaiting the coming of day.

Presently he arose and quietly unfastening the chain, he slipped the miniature back again about the child's throat—with trembling, yet loving hands.

"Ours for eternity, Little Son!" he whispered softly—and his heart was full of the Christmas peace.

SOCIAL PSYCHOLOGY.

Social phychology is the study of the psychic planes and currents that come into existence among men in consequence of their association. It neglects the uniformities among people that are produced by the direct action of a common physical environment, and the uniformities arising directly or indirectly out of race endowment, and deals only with those due to mental causes, i. e., to mental contacts or mental interactions.

Social psychology seeks to enlarge our knowledge of society by explaining how so many planes in feeling, belief or purpose have established themselves among men and supplied a basis for their groupings, their coöperations, and their conflicts. Every individual's mind and actions are influenced by his social surroundings. One's mind cannot develop unless it is acted upon by other minds. Stimuli welling up from within may be called impulses, whereas those reaching us directly from without may be termed suggestions. Suggestions may be defined as "the abrupt entrance from without into consciousness of an idea or image which becomes a part of the stream of thought, and tends to produce the muscular and volitional efforts which ordinarily follow upon its presence." Suggestions are true forces and enact themselves unless they meet resistance. Children's minds are plastic and hence offer the least resistance to suggestions.

People are more open to suggestibility when they are fasting, absent minded and fatigued. In the normal mental state, indirect suggestion succeeds best, in the abnormal state, direct suggestion

One is most susceptible to suggestions from certain quarters or 'rom certain people—those clothed with prestige. Prestige is that which excites such wonder or admiration as to paralyze the critical 'aculty. It is not the same for all stages of personal or racial development. To the boy, his ideal is probably some general or hero. As he grows older his ideals change. One must show his power and force in order to gain prestige.

Suggestibility is contagious. No matter how strong one's own convictions may be, they will finally be overcome by the common sentiment of the crowd. In a crowd there is the fixation of attention, excitement, expectancy and a narrowing of the field of consciousness, that excludes disturbing impressions. An excited throng easily turns mob, because excitement weakens the reasoning powers.

Feelings, having more means of vivid expression run through the crowd more readily than ideas. Boisterous laughter, frantic cheers, and gesticulations are needed to express the feelings and sentiment of the crowd. Such exaggerated signs of emotion cannot but produce exaggerated states of mind.

In a real deliberative assembly, the best thought, place, or soundest opinion will prevail. Where there is deliberation, the best deas are approved and accepted by all. In a crowd, the leader may be as frantic as any, and thus the utmost folly prevail.

Under these conditions—heightened suggestibility and emoion, arrested thinking,—three things will happen when an impulse, whether emanating from a spectacle, an event or a leader, runs hrough the crowd.

1st Extension. By sheer contagion it spreads through the rowd to unsympathetic persons, who against their will are drawn nto the sentiment of the crowd.

2nd Intensification. When each individual impressed sees hat others share his same emotions, the intensity of his own feelngs is increased and thus that of the whole crowd.

3rd Predisposition. The perceived unison begets a sympathy hat makes like response easier the next time. The passing of the rowd into the mob is more or less gradual. A mob is a formation hat takes time. A revivalist expects little response the first half our. It takes time to work the minds up to a certain pitch. After this it is easy. The people are swayed against their will, and are unconsciously drawn along with the mass in sentiment.

The crowd cannot last. The straining and attention lead to fatigue. Then stimuli from within help to break the spell. Sensations of hunger, cold and weariness become so insistent as to distract the attention. Presently the spell is broken and the crowd scatters.

The crowd is always unstable. It may pass from reckless courage to fear. A word or action may turn its whole purpose. It is also irrational. In its madness it does not judge or reflecct. It is immoral and is the lowest form of association. Right conduct is thought-out conduct and since thronging paralyzes thought and while the crowd may be sentimental and heroic, it will lack the virtues born of self-control—veracity, prudence, thrift, perseverance, respect for another's rights and obedience to law.

Mob mind may exist without a crowd. In these days of newspapers, the telegraph and telephone, news is quickly spread over all parts of the country. Our space-annihilating devices make a shock well nigh simultaneous. The true crowd is in a declining role. Universal contact by means of print ushers in "the rule of public opinion" which is a totally different thing from "government by the mob."

The principal manifestations of mob mind in vast bodies of dispersed individuals are the craze and the fad. As in the typical mob there must be a center which radiates impulses by fascination till they have subdued enough people to continue their course by sheer intimidation, so for the craze there must be an excitant, overcoming so many people that these can affect the rest by mere volume of suggestion. The starting point may be produced by some striking event or incident. The murder of a leader, the insult to an ambassador, the advent of a railroad, the failure of a bank, a number of deaths by an epidemic, an earth quake, all these have resulted in some fever, mania, crusade, boom, panic, delusion or fright. The laws of crazes may be formulated as follows:

1. The craze takes time to develop to its height.

2. The more extensive its ravages, the stronger the type of intellect that falls a prey to it.

3. The greater its height the more absurd the propositions that will be believed or the actions that will be done.

4. The higher the craze, the sharper the reaction from it.

5. One craze is frequently succeeded by another, exciting emotions of a different character.

6. A dynamic society is more craze-ridden than one moving along the ruts of custom.

The fad originates in the surprise or interest excited by novelty. Roller skating, blue glass, a forty days' fast, faith healing, telepathy are all fads. No department of life is safe from the invasion of novelty. Thus we have all kinds of fads: philosophic fads, like pessimism or anarchism; literary fads, religious fads, hygenic, medical and personal fads. Time is the test whether a novelty is a reality or a fad.

Fashion is somewhat akin to novelty or fad. It springs from a desire to individualize one's self from one's fellows. Progress follows the line of advantage, substituting always the better adapted. Fashion on the other hand moves in cycles. Fashion consists of imitation and differentiation. In imitation, the inferior asserts his equality with the superior by copying him in externals. The superiors resent this and immediately change the style. The terms "gentleman" and "lady" are abandoned as soon as common people employ them profusely. There it is remarked how "noble" are the ancient terms "man" and "woman." Conformity to the fashionable style is more prompt and general than formerly, and the changes of fashion are more frequent. As soon as a thing can be imitated in an inferior quality, and thus become accessible to all, the fashion changes. The growth of intelligence causes the desire for self-individualization to seek satisfaction in other ways than fashion. Much can be done by association in dress reform. Reform will probably come, not by the general adoption of some costume in flat contrast to fashionable apparel, but by adding to the number of occasions on which rational costumes already devised may be worn.

"By conventionality is meant a psychic plane resulting from the deliberate, non-competitive, non-rational imitation of contemporaries." These qualifying terms differentiate it respectively from the psychic planes laid by mob mind, fashion, rational imitation and custom. Conventionality reaches to the very framework of our lives. Prestige of opinion governs our actions. People have come to believe that pecuniary success is the only success. The upper classes, or the elite, set the standard of society. Thus it has come about that things are considered beautiful in proportion as they are costly. Women, instead of finding for themselves the right adjustment to life, follow male opinion as to what is proper and womanly.

According to the laws of conventionality imitation, motor impulses appear to diffuse themselves with great facility. This is one reason why the fervor and excitement of revivals reach such a pitch. We are most imitative in things that are not the objects of conscious attention. We unconsciously acquire a brogue or new expressions of speech. The itch of curiosity is communicable.

Although generally the social superior is imitated by the social inferior, the social superior sometimes borrows from the inferior. The Southerners copy the negroes in their speech, and homely country phrases flavor city speech. The lower classes may copy their ancestors rather than their superiors. Certain conditions of life make this recommendable.

A society of equals tends to stagnate unless education, both lower and higher, is amply provided for. Education lifts men above the common plane and gives them high ideals and aspirations. In England the peers and lords are considered much above the scientists, artists and literary men. The English ideal is pleasure, rank and wealth. England can never be free, wholesome, and whole-souled until she has cast out these ideals. In all conditions of society the one with power, honor and prestige is imitated.

By custom is meant the transmission of a way of doing; by tradition is meant the transmission of a way of thinking or believing. Here custom will be used in the wider sense as any transmission of psychic elements from one generation to another. Children must associate with their parents in order to transmit customs. In whatever way a man has done a thing once, he has a tendency to do it again, and also a tendency to make others do the same, and transmits his formed customs to his children by teaching and example. There is a difference between heredity and custom. We inherit only from ancestors, but in childhood we imitate the one salient copy, whether it is the example of a parent or of another. There is a tendency for the transmitted to become even more definite and precise, so that each generation is confined under a thicker and tougher cake of custom.

One reason why people adhere to old customs is partly due to fear of the spirits of the deceased forefathers. What is received becomes fixed by habit and so becomes more obdurate with advancing years. Thus society will be conservative or progressive according as it puts to the fore old men or young men. Physical isolation favors the sway of custom. In mountain regions the old endures long after the new has been accepted in open and accessible places. Social isolation by hindering contact with contemporaries, makes closer the contact with the past. Jews, penned up in the Ghetto and barred from social and civil equality, came to be obstinately traditional. Open discussion, reading and warfare break the bonds of custom and give the individuals a wider scope. Family ties and traditions bind custom.

In open discussion there is sure to be differences of opinion, and these most fiercely fought. These differences of opinion should be well thrashed out until an agreement is reached, which should settle the matter not temporarily, but for all time. Talk, sentiment and the press are best able to bring about a compromise. Controversy is profitless unless it has a common basis. It must appeal to reason, rather than to passion and prejudice. Some struggles last indefinitely because of inborn differences between human beings. Some may end by the extinction of one side by the other, or by their coming together on a common ground. But no controversy is settled until it is settled right.

Alice L. Darrah, '11.

JERUSHA JANE'S CHRISTMAS.

Jerusha Jane stopped short in the midst of her biscuit making, and brought one flour-covered fist down heavily upon the table. "Those people shall have a Christmas, if I have to die for it," she said, and departed cheerfully to get a cloth with which to wipe up the flour she had spilled by her vehement blow.

Then the biscuit baking went on with renewed vigor. When at last the biscuits emerged from the oven, deliciously browned, Jerusha aimed them angrily at a plate, thereby spilling them to the four corners of the farm house kitchen.

"What people don't know, doesn't hurt them," she remarked philosophically stooping to pick them up.

"One, two, three, four, five! No more and no less!" she said shortly, as she aimed them again at the plate, this time singly, and with better success. "Such closeness is beyond human endurance. Nine years, I've skimped out three meagre meals a day for these three women. And never an extra bite has been cooked. Just enough to go once around—any more would be wasteful, says Miss Sally, sour old maid that she is. I thank Heaven that even if I am unmarried, I haven't quite dried up like her, and Miss Annie, and Miss Lou. Among them all poor Miss Jean is hardly allowed to breathe. But they'll have a Christmas, as sure as my name's Jerusha Jane Williams."

With that, she called the family to their evening meal of biscuits, jam and coffee. The three maiden ladies filed in together, solemnly, as was their custom.

"Jean is not coming this evening," Jerusha," said Miss Sally. "I intended to tell you, so you would only need to make four biscuits. This is sinful waste." She did not notice Jerusha's wrye face as she went out, or hear her muttered remark that "It was a good thing Miss Jean got out occasionally to get a good filling up. The poor thing didn't get enough at home to keep her alive. The only reason the others lived was because they were so much 'dried up,' it didn't take much to keep them."

Jerusha was longer than usual in clearing up, that night, and when she finally made her way to her attic room her step was noticealy stealthy.

She heard Jean, the young miece come in at about eleven. She lay awake for some time listening to the sobbing in the little room across the hall. How well Jerusha knew the reason of those tears. Just a little over a year ago Jean's mother had died, and the home with these maiden aunts seemed a mere mockery of her former one. They "meant well" by her, but understood her little.

After that life went on much the same as usual. The only difference the three aunts noticed was that Jerusha's crustiness seemed to have vanished entirely. Yes, and there were other things that vanished. Miss Anne noticed that the eggs, which were her especial care, were constantly decreasing in number. And Miss Sally missed two of her nicest turkeys which she had been sure would bring a good price at Christmas. And Miss Sou noticed that the amount of sugar in the sugar barrel was daily fast growing less. Countless other disappearances in the stores led to the belief that some tramp was living off the proceeds of their farm. Every precaution was taken, but the things still vanished.

"It's too bad to deprive Jean of a Christmas," remarked Miss Lou one day, wistfully.

"Nonsense, Louisa. The discipline of doing without will do her far more good than a great celebration," said Miss Sally emphatically. Whereupon Miss Lou subsided into silence.

Christmas morning dawned—an ideal day, crisply cold, with just enough snow for sleighing sparkling under the winter sun.

Jerusha was awakened by a gentle tap at her door. She opened it for Jean to enter softly with a little package in her hand.

"Merry Christmas, dear Jerusha, though there isn't much to make it so," she whispered. "This is all I have for you, but it had to be done after night. You know what my aunts think about gift giving."

"It's lovely, dearie, and so acceptable," said Jerusha unrolling a neatly hemstitched linen handkerchief.

"Sorry I haven't anything for you but good wishes," she added. She did not look sorry in the least; her face fairly beamed.

After the usual breakfast the aunts and Jean drove off to church at the village, five miles away. As Miss Sallie always celebrated the day by visiting the poor and sick, Jerusha knew she need hardly expect them back before one o'clock.

As soon as the sleigh was safely out of hearing, all became hurry and bustle within the farmhouse. The farm hands were called in to help. In the "best" room a great wood fire was kindled and the chandelier and mantel were hung with Christmas greens which Jerusha had smuggled home from market the day before. The "big" dining room was opened up and aired, and the "best" tablecloth spread upon the table. All the while the most savory odors came from the region of the kitchen.

By and by the door bell began to ring frequently and queer little giggles and murmurs came from the "best" room.

Then a jingling sleigh drove into the yard, from which Jean alighted, assisted by a handsome youth, who, much to her alarm, announced his intention of coming in. With a mental picture of the cold dreary best room, she opened the door, about to show him in. She stopped short in the doorway, then with a little cry of delight ran about from one person to another. For the room was filled with neighbors—young and old. And way over in the corner sat the deacon—Aunt Sallie's old "beau" who hadn't spoken to her for years.

"Jerusha! Jerusha! You're the biggest dear that ever lived," Jean exclaimed, running back to the kitchen to hug her.

The aunts, when they arrived a little later, were no less astonished. A faint glow of pleasure rose to the faces of the sisters, especially to that of Miss Sally as she greeted the deacon.

That was a wonderful Christmas. Never had the old house held such a merry crowd. Seldom had it seen served so bountiful a dinner. And never had there been within it so many hearts brimful of happiness.

"Jerusha Jane Williams," said Jean as she was going to bed, "you have achieved a triumph. The aunts have decided that Christmas should be celebrated, also that they have held aloof from people much too long; Aunt Sallie is going to marry Deacon Lee, at last!"

"Well, I'm heartily glad I did it," said Jerusha. "I've lied and stolen, and perjured my soul, I suppose, but I'm glad I—did—it."

And Jean only hugged her.

Florence Kerr Wilson, '11.

THOMPSON'S "SHELLEY."

It is not often that a poet is so fortunate as to have for his critic another poet, and one of like mind with himself. Shelley has this advantage in Thompson's essay. As one might suppose, there is great sympathy with the subject. If faults are criticised they are criticised by a friend who sees deeper than the deed into the heart.

To Thompson, Shelly had the heart of a child. "Know you what it is to be a child? . . . It is to have a spirit yet streaming from the waters of baptism; it is to believe in love, to believe in loveliness, to believe in belief; it is to be so little that the elves can reach to whisper in your ear; it is to turn pumpkins into coaches, and mice into horses, lowness into loftiness, and nothing into everything, for each child has its fairy godmother in its own soul." .

This childlikiness in Shelley appears in his grief over imaginary sorrows, in his amusements, and in the inconsistency and restlessness of his life.

We see it again in his poetry, with its perfect spontaneity and unaffectedness. In his songs "the childs faculty of make-believe is raised to the m-th power. He is still at play, save only that his play is such as manhood stops to watch, and his play things are those which the gods give their children. The universe is his box of toys. He dabbles his fingers in the day-fall. He is gold-dusty with trembling amidst the stars. He makes bright mischief with the moon. The meteors muzzle their noses in his hand. He teases into growling the kennelled thunder, and laughs at the shaking of its fiery chain. He dances in and out of the gates of heaven: its floor is littered with his broken fancies. He runs wild over the fields of ether. He chases the rolling world. He gets between the feet of the horses of the sun. He stands in the lap of patient Nature, and twines her loosened tresses after a hundred wilful fashions, to see how she will look nicest in his song."

This sympathy of Thompson's is especially shown in his treatment of the evil side of Shelley's life. "We see clearly that he committed grave sins and one cruel crime; but we remember also that he was an atheist from his boyhood; we reflect how gross must have been the moral neglect in the training of a child who could be an atheist from his boyhood, and we decline to judge so unhappy a being by the rule which we should apply to a Catholic." Shelley was weakly blindly struggling against this, as is shown by the fact that he grew out of atheism into Paultheism which is a step on the higher road.

The essay is itself a poem. In its beautiful, forceful language and metaphors, and most of all in its spirit, it is all poetry. Instead of bringing to our minds a blue book with a gilt binding containing a picture of a poet and his works, we have been taught to love and sympathize with a passionate, burning, beautiful being.

Mary D. Lindsay.

THE FOREST RING.

Far in the Forest,
  When day is done,
And darkness has swallowed
  The evening sun,—
There, where the katydids
  Fiddle and sing,
The fairies disport in
  A magical ring.

Moonlight of silver
  On velvety green
Cloaks in a mystery
  The sprightly scene,
The owl stops complaining
  To gaze in a trance
On the wee spirits swinging
  In rythmical dance.

Moonbeams of silver
  Soon steal far away,
The dew becomes cold
  In the dawning of day,
Then under the oak leaves
  The fairy folk spring,
And 'twas only a dream
  Of the magical ring.

Minerva Hamilton, '11.

THE CIRCUS.

"Well, Dot, I suppose you want to go to the circus tomorrow," said Dot's father, as the family seated themselves at breakfast, and Dot promptly made it known that she was wild to go. All little girls enjoy a circus, especially the "Greatest Show on Earth". "Business is pressing just now, but I think I can manage, somehow, to get away for half a day. I don't want you to miss it."

"Why, John, I am going to take Dot to the show, of course. I supposed you would know that," spoke up grandfather with an injured air. "I don't mind giving up one afternoon for the dear child's pleasure."

"But I can get off very well, father. Thompson won't object. Of course though if you want to come along—"

"The idea! here are two busy men squabbling about who is to take Dot to the circus, when it is understood that I am going with her," interrupted Aunt Mary, sharply. "My time is not as valuable as yours. I hate the dirty, greasy circus people and the whole thing is disgusting, but it is a pity if I can't sacrifice my own feelings for the child's pleasure."

"If you put it that way," Uncle Harry broke in, "I see that it is my duty to go, too. Lots of fun Dot would have with you people. I wager she wouldn't get a drop of pink lemonade or a peep at the Greatest Living Wonder. But I know the ins and outs of a circus, and it is plainly my duty to give Dot a royal good time."

The next day as mother watched the company of five walking down the street she remarked with a discreet smile, "How interested they are in that child!"

Lillian McHenry, '13.

THE SOROSIS
Published Monthly by the Students of
Pennsylvania College for Women.

Ethel Tassey, '10..............................Editor-in-Chief
Elma McKibben, '10..........................Business Manager
Minerva Hamilton, '11..........................Literary Editor
Elvira Estep, '12..............................College Notes
Calla Stahlman, '12................................Personals
Marguerite Frey, '13..............................Exchanges
Gertrude Wayne, '11................Assistant Business Manager

Subscriptions to the Sorosis, 75 cents per year. Single copies, 10c.
Address all business communications to the Business Manager.
Entered in the Postoffice at Pittsburg, Pa., as second-class matter.

EDITORIAL

"Christmas Gift!" This was the cry according to an old Irish custom, with which neighbor was wont to greet neighbor on Christmas morning, whether at a chance meeting or on a morning call. The one who spoke first was entitled to a gift from the other. These simple words seem to express the key note of the average attitude today toward the celebration of December 25th. The gift is apparently the all-important thing. Much has been said in the last few years concerning the question of Christmas giving. As the season approaches new arguments are added to the old against the lengths to which this custom has gone. It is true the idea may be traced to the First Christmas But our version of it suffers much in comparison with the original.

The problem has become most perplexing to the girl at school. When she enters this new phase of her life, she rushes into many new friendships which, though sudden, are often strong and lasting. Naturally at the holiday season she adds the new names to her list of relatives and friends wishing to remember them all and appropriately. But her wishes are not all that need consulting.

"Ay, that's the rub!"

If she is wise, her own experience will soon teach her that the will truly stands for the deed and instead of tormenting herself and the family with an impossible problem, she will grasp one of the numerous opportunities offered in this age of cleverness of simply and sincerely wishing all, as the Sorosis does, a Merry, Merry Christmas.

"Don't forget the Short Story Contest.

SHORT STORY CONTEST ! ! !

The "Sorosis" announces a short story contest, open to all College students. A prize of $5.00 will be awarded for the best story handed to the Editors before January 10, 1910. Manuscripts must be written on one side only.

ALUMNAE.

Several of the Alumnae were present at the concert on Friday evening, December third. Among those present were Miss Bessie Johnson, Miss Ellen McKee and Miss Jennie McSherry.

Mr. and Mrs. Walter Dann were the guests of Miss Kerst last Friday evening at dinner and later at the concert.

On Saturday, December fourth, Miss Coburn was hostess at a luncheon for several members of the Alumnae and present college students. After luncheon the girls spent the rest of the afternoon dressing dolls for the Kindergarten Association.

Several interesting letters have been received from Miss Coulter. She is enjoying the social life and hospitality of the south.

Miss Ruth Johnston, '03, is teaching science this year at Milwaukee Downer College.

Miss Clara Niebaum, '07, has accepted a position in Vandergrift High School.

A little daughter was born to Mr. and Mrs. Charles Searing, '02, in November.

Miss Hilda Sadler has returned from New York where she has been visiting during the past month.

Miss Lyda Young, who has been spending a few weeks in Chicago, stopped on her way home and visited Mrs. Coleman (nee Mary Wilson, '03). Miss Anna Wilson is now visiting Mrs. Coleman.

The Decade II Club held its November meeting at the home of Mrs. John Houston, Murray Hill avenue. After the program most of the afternoon was occupied in the dressing of dolls for the charity association.

The December meeting of the Decade II Club will be held at the home of Miss Anna Houston, Pacific avenue. The members will take up the study of "Latest Essays" by modern authors.

COLLEGE NOTES.

The members of the school and their friends were given a treat on Friday evening, November twenty-sixth, when Mr. Whitmer, our new musical director, played parts from the music Debussy has written to Maeterlinck's "Peleas and Mellisande." He was assisted by Miss Kerst who read the fourth and fifth acts.

On Wednesday morning, December first, Mr. Kiernan gave a reading of Rip Van Winkle before the students of the College and Dilworth Hall. Mr. Kiernan knew Joseph Jefferson personally, and gave us Mr. Jefferson's interpretation of the play. Everybody thoroughly enjoyed the reading.

Senior-Junior night was held by the Dramatic Club on Friday evening, December tenth, when the Seniors produced, "A Song at the Castle", and the Juniors, "The Ladies of Cranford."

The following was the cast of "A Song at the Castle":

Cornwallis .... Mary Kramer
Desmond O'Moirne .... Gladwin Coburn
Col. Humphrey Morton .... Rachel McQuiston

Sir Richard Wilde............................Lucille Shurmer
Marquis Raoul de la Valiere.........................Eva Cohen
A. Servant..................................Mary Lindsay
Lady Wyndham...............................Ethel Tassey
Eileen Fitzgerald...........................Elma McKibben

Time—Early evening of a night in July, 1798.

Place—Dublin Castle; the state drawing room.

The Cranford cast included:

Miss Matilda Jenkyns................Sara Reynolds Carpenter
Miss Mary Smith....................Gertrude Jeannette Wayne
Miss Jessie Brown....................Maggie May McCollough
Miss Pole............................Mabel Florence Crowe
Mrs. Forrester.....................Margaret Katherine Greene
Miss Betty Barker..................Francesca Alden Cameron
The Hon. Mrs. Jamieson................Rosalie Printz Supplee
Mrs. Fritz-Adams.......................Florence Kerr Wilson
Lady Glenmire............................Elma Marie Trussell
Martha ....Alice Lillian Darrah
Peggy...............................Minerva Jane Hamilton
Mrs. Purkis............................Rita Clarissa Blakeslee
Peter Marmaduke Arley Jenkns........Belle Vance McClymouds

Act I—Scene, Miss Matty's Parlor—Afternoon Tea.

Act II—Scene, Same—"Miss Matilda Jenkyns' licensed to sell tea."

Act III—Scene, Miss Barker's Parlor—A Card Party.

Great interest is being taken in the annual college Christmas dinner which is to be given Thursday, December sixteenth, the evening before school closes, and preparations are already being made. Names have been drawn for the joke-gifts and each table commitee is working hard with the determination to have its table arranged the prettiest and the most original.

The college girls are looking forward to a Christmas dance to be given in the pretty dining room of South Hall. Committees have been appointed and arrangements are in full swing, promising to make the affair a success in every way.

The Social Service classes under Miss Meloy accepted a special invitation to hear a lecture by Dr. Hart, of the Russell Sage Foundation, given in the Chamber of Commerce rooms in the Keenan Building. A social time and refreshments closed the program of the evening.

The Faculty teas have been somewhat varied lately. On Tuesday afternoon, November twenty-third, Mr. Putnam and Mr. Martin were hosts at a "Smoker" at which the usual refreshments were served. But somehow the ladies didn't object. Mr. Whitmer gave a musical tea, each guest took the opportunity to have her voice tested.

Dr. Lindsay and Miss Coolidge attended the exercises with which Dr. W. W. Foster, Jr., was inaugurated President of Beaver College, Tuesday, November sixteenth. A unique feature of the occasion was the Academic procession from the college building to the church in which the services were held. Lights were placed at intervals along the line of march and the students sang college songs and gave their yells.

After the opening exercises addresses were made by Bishop J. W. Hamilton, Rev. Arthur Staples and Bishop W. F. Anderson. Dr. Foster was then formally installed as President of Beaver College and delivered his inaugural address. At the suggestion of Bishop Anderson the audience gave Dr. Foster the Chautauqua salute and Bishop Anderson closed the services with the benediction.

PERSONALS.

The college girls have discovered that they have some fine cooks among their number.

Miss Diescher, Junior, recently sat very quietly for about fifteen minutes during a recitation in Current History, thinking she was listening to a German lesson. These Juniors.

Mrs. Armstrong spent her Thanksgiving vacation at her home in Vandergrift, Pa. Miss Edna McKee accompanied her.

Miss Evelyn Crandall was at her home inWarren, Pa., over Thanksgiving.

Miss Ionia Smith spent a pleasant vacation at her home in Clarksburg, W. Va.

Mrs. J. B. Smith visited her daughter, Ionia, during the "College Teas".

Miss Clarissa Blakeslee rusticated near Clarion during the recent holidays and participated in some rural products.

A new interpretation of Calvin's doctrine given by Miss Wilson:—Baptism is not necessary for damnation

Some of the South Hall girls are making rapid progress in forethought. One was even thoughtful enough to take her ticket with her to the theater one night.

Miss Marion Knapp was the guest of the Senior class Friday evening, December tenth, and attended the plays given by the Juniors and Seniors. Miss Knapp is the honorary member of the class of '10.

Miss Susan McLean is sojourning at Colorado Springs during the winter.

Dr. Lindsay has returned from a two-weeks' stay in Asheville, N. C., where Mrs. Lindsay is spending the winter. Mrs. Lindsay is very much improved in health.

Announcement has been made of the engagement of Miss Edith Clarke, formerly of Boston to Mr. George W. Putnam. The wedding is to take place in December.

Miss Ruth Peck leaves Thursday, December sixteenth, to spend the holidays with her parents in Concordia, Kansas, and also to participate in the wedding of her sister, Margaret, to Mr. William Theron Wright. Miss Margaret Peck is a former Dilworth Hall student.

Y. W. C. A.

At the weekly meeting of the Y. W. C. A. Tuesday, November thirtieth, the members were divided into classes which are to take up different phases of Bible study during the remainder of the year. Miss Mary Lindsay and Miss Mary Brindsmade conduct a class in Home Mission Study, Miss Meloy assisted by Miss McKibben a class in the Social Teachings of Christ, and Miss Maude Demmler teaches a class in the study of the Life of Christ.

The annual bazaar was not. But one of its biggest attractions, the doll show, was held as usual in the drawing rooms on the afternoon of Friday, December tenth. This great fashion show has long been famous for its wonderful creations and this one was certainly not an exception. These dolls were dressed by the girls for distribution at the free kindergartens.

MUSIC NOTES.

We received one of the most delightful treats of the year on the evening of December third, in Mme Grasiani's first recital. Mme Grasiani's charming personality had endeared her to all her pupils long before, but on that night she won the hosts of visitors as her friends.

Her recital contained examples of the highest German Lieder and English and American song. Both German and English songs were sung with genuine artistry, and were thoroughly enjoyed.

Mr. Von Kunitz is well known to all Pittsburghers, and his popularity was shown in the enthusiastic manner in which he was received. He played with the highest skill and finish.

Mrs. Clare Ward Humphrey has taken Miss Drais' place in the musical faculty.

The Christmas music, consisting of both old and modern carols of different countries, will be given on the morning of Wednesday, the fifteenth of December. The Glee Club are working on special music for the occasion.

"Do you mean to say that two and two make five is right?"
"Well, it's four-fifths right, ain't it?

A witty woman has coined the word "muncheon" to describe one of Fletcher's feasts.

Beggar: "My parents died and left me an orphan."
"They did, eh? Well, what are you going to do with it?"—Life.

Mother may I go study bridge,
Yes, my darling Mable,
Learn all the rules you can by heart
But don't go near the table.
—Harper's Weekly.

Pat got a job moving some kegs of powder and to the alarm of the foreman, was discovered smoking at his work.

"Gracious," exclaimed the foreman. "Do you know what happened when a man smoked at this job some years ago? There was an explosion which blew up a dozen men."

"That couldn't happen here," returned Pat, calmly.

"Why not?"

"'Cos there's only me and you," was the reply.

Contemporary Fiction.

Visitor—"What have you in arctic literature?"
Librarian—"Cook books and Peary odicals."—Ex.

Monsieur—Can you translate into French the words "our sisters?"

Little Tommy (stammering)—"No, sir."

Monsieur—That's right.

OMEGA SOCIETY.

Thursday afternoon, December first, the society met in the reception room. The annual election of officers was held, Rosalie Supplee, '11, being chosen President and Irma E. Diescher, '11, Secretary and Treasurer. After the business meeting the following program was carried out:

Paper—"Life of Frank R. Stockton"............Mary Kramer, '10
Paper—"The Late Mrs. Null"..................Mabel Crowe, '11
Paper—"The Casting Away of Mrs. Leeks and Mrs. Aleshine" ....Minerva Hamilton, '11

After interested discussion of Mr. Stockton and his work, the society adjourned with the singing of the Omega song.

EXCHANGES.

"The Olio" from Marietta College, is one of our best exchanges for November. The "Lesbian Herald" is also good.

"A Pansy."

Fair white, with tints of palest blue,
A pansy face, with heart of gold.
Only a flower? Yes, but it told
A thought to me, a message new.

The blue is for the faith of you,
The white for peace and purity,
The golden heart—oh, that, you see,
Speaks of your love so great, so true!

—Ex.

"Crushes."

You ask me what you have to do?
Well, really, I don't know.
You buy her flowers and candy,
As though you were her beau.

And then you follow her about
And—please don't ask me more!
This will discourage you, no doubt,
But sometimes, they're a bore!

—Ex.

Nephew (just returned from abroad)—"This franc-piece, Aunt, I got in Paris."

Aunt Hepsey—"I wish, nephew, you'd bring home one a them Latin quarters they talk about so much."—Ex.

The November number of "The Magnet" is well gotten-up.

Mr. B.—"To what nationality do Dr. Cook and Commander eary belong?"
Mr. Y.—"Pole-landers!"—Ex.

"What have you in the shape of bananas?" asked a customer the new grocery clerk.
"Nothing but cucumbers, sir!"—Ex.

"Mein Gott! Mein Gott! Ich hab' forgot,
Und left in meinen Zimmer,
Mein liebes, bestes, deutschen "Trot"
Recitieren kann ich nimmer!"
—Ex.

Prof.—"How does this poem rank with the others, under dis- ussion?"
Answer—"It's as rank as the rest."—Ex.

"Freshmen to Their Geometry Texts"
How can I bear to close thee!
One parting glance I give thee!
For when I hear him call me,
I fear what doom befall me:
Farewell, farewell, my own true text!
Farewell, farewell, my own true text!
—Ex.

THE SOROSIS

VOL. XVI JANUARY, 1910 No. 3

CLAYTON'S DEBUTANTE.

The Lafferty family was peacefully seated around the large sitting-room table. That is, if the quiet which reigned there could be called peace. Mrs. Lafferty had for some moments been clearing her throat at intervals, which filled the hearts of Patrick, her husband, and Mary Ann, her daughter, with ominous forebodings. At length she began:

"Patrick Lafferty, aint I for twenty——"

"Don't say 'ain't,' mother!" put in Mary Ann as she poked the coal fire unconcernedly.

"Now, chip in, you little snipe! I ain't had no thousands spent on my eddication, so a course I can't allus speak grammatic." Mary Ann had lately graduated from a finishing school, "eddicated", as her mother expressed it, "to be a regular lady."

"Well, as I was sayin', Patrick O'Reilly Lafferty, haven't I llus done everything to make you comfortable and happy! And ere ye are, never doin' a thing for a body in the way of gettin' me nter Sassiety."

"Well, Ma, what ye drivin' at?" asked Patrick, as he squirmed uneasily in his seat. "What do ye want now? Spit it out, and e'll git it!"

"I want to see my name in the Sassiety columns of the 'Clayon News'—I want to give somethin' real swell, and I been thinkin' n' thinkin'. Now there's Mary Ann, she'd arter be interduced, as were, to our friends."

"Why, woman, they've all known her since she was a squallin' aby! Interduce her!" and Patrick laughed that superior aggravatng laugh, which only a man can laugh.

"Just the same, Pat Lafferty, she's going to be my debuttant aughter Marie Antoinette Lafferty, interduced at a beautifully apointed tay, given at the residence of her father."

"But mother, my name's not Marie Antoinette. It's plain Mary Ann, and there's no use introducing me, and I won't."

"Oh, yes ye will," came sternly from her father. "What yer mother says around this ranch goes. When are ye thinkin' of havin' yer shindig?"

From that time on, Mary Ann to the contrary, preparations for the "shindig" went on. After a hard struggle she succeeded in having her name left as it was, with only the addition of an "e" on the Anne. But introduced to the society of Clayton she must be.

Clayton, be it known, was distinctly a mining town. Patrick himself had been a miner before he struck "ile" which elevated him to the position of Clayton's wealthiest citizen. But the glitter of wealth had never affected him to the length that he forgot his old friends. On the contrary, he was a "friend in need" to all of them.

No matter how much of dread lay in the acceptance of Mrs. Lafferty's invitation, every one of the miner's wives would have accepted it or died in the attempt. They did not quite know what it meant. "To introduce her daughter Mary Anne" when they all knew her already? Oh well, they would wait and see. Meanwhile the inevitable feminine bugbear of what to wear, was uppermost in the minds of the women of Clayton.

At the biggest house in Clayton, preparations went on apace. Mrs. Lafferty was as much at a loss to know how Mary Anne was to be introduced to Clayton society as were the recipients of the invitations themselves. What would she do with her guests when she had them there? Mary Anne could help her little. Somehow at the fashionable school, she had never been "in things". Her experience there had been a slow period of torture, suffered in the cause of "sassiety," at the instigation of Mary Ann's mother.

The eventful day dawned much the same as other days not singled out for so portentious an occasion. Mrs. Lafferty had decided that "The hostess and her daughter were receiving at the foot of the stairs surrounded by palms" would sound very well indeed in the society columns of the Clayton News. So the palms were banked for this artistic effect at the place mentioned. Mary Anne's new gown was elaborate, but pretty. To dress tastefully was one thing at least, that her education had taught her. Her chief efforts since her graduation had been to tone down her mother's barbarous love for bright colors, and to correct her murderous abuses of the Queen's English.

At two o'clock the two, mother and daughter, equally overcome with dread, stationed themselves amid the before mentioned palms. Patrick came in to look them over.

"Ye'll do, both of ye," he said meekly encouraging them. "Now I spose I've gotta light out. This is no place for me. Good luck to ye." And he disappeared from view.

Mrs. Michael Finnegan was the first arrival. The servant (hired for the occasion), asked for her name. She, being known ordinarily to the Laffertys as "Sally," was rather taken aback. After repeating her name loudly, the servant led her to the foot of the stairs. Awed beyond measure, she attempted to greet her friend Jane Lafferty in the usual manner. But a look from that dignified matron quickly silenced her.

"Mrs. Finnegan," she said, extending the tips of her fat gloved fingers, at which the lady addressed looked very blank, "I want you to meet my daughter, Mary Anne. This is Mrs. Finnegan, my dear."

"But la! Jane, I know Mary Anne. What ye doin' this for? Has money turned yer head complately?"

"Sally Finnegan! That there's rank slander!" said the good lady. "You're a nasty ongrateful crature to come to my house and accept of my bounty, and then tell me to my face that money has turned my head!" Mrs. Lafferty grew red with righteous indignation.

"Mother, mother, Mrs. Finnegan meant nothing. Come back and stand with me," pleaded Mary Anne, tugging at her mother's sleeve. Mrs. Lafferty, however, having her temper roused, forgot everything but her rage, and carried on a heated argument with Mrs. Finnegan unmindful that in her haste she had departed from the carefully placed palms.

How the women, from such a small beginning ever thought of so many cruel things to say to one another, only a woman can know. When Mrs. Lafferty's voice was strained to the highest squeak, and Mrs. Finnegan's was at the breaking point, Mrs. Daniel Dougall and Miss Alva Dougall were announced.

Despite Mary Anne's cheerful attempts to keep them interested they soon discovered the ladies and their difficulty.

No one knew how it came about, but in a short time the ladies were discussing a new cherry preserve quietly and amiably, and the girls were sitting on the stairs exchanging confidences.

Dignity and airs were forgotten and by the time the next arrivals came, the fact that Mary Anne was to be introduced was completely overlooked—much to the joy of that meek little person. The refined elegant "tay" turned into one of the rousing good times to which the crowd were accustomed, and when Patrick arrived, as was his habit, with most of the Clayton men to eat up the "lawin's", the gayety was at its height. Then the afternoon "tay" lengthened itself into a dinner-dance, and each and every participant went home after "the time of his or her life."

"I'm mighty glad mother and Mrs. Finnegan did fight," whispered Mary Anne to Tom McHenry, known to the inhabitants of Clayton as "Mary's young man."

"And you're just the same, even if you have debutted," he smiled back at her.

The press notice the next morning was not even one bitter drop in the Lafferty's cup of joy. For hadn't it been written before Mrs. Finnegan came with her blessed old row? And so it stands on the ineffacable records of Clayton:—

"At a beautifully appointed tea Mrs. P. Lafferty yesterday introduced her daughter, Mary Anne, to Clayton society. The hostess and her daughter stood at the foot of the stairs, receiving, surrounded by palms."

The very words! What more could any one ask?

Florence Kerr Wilson, '11.

"PSYCHOLOGY OF SPEECH BASED ON EVOLUTION."

Almost everything now seems to go through a series of evolution or as it was formerly expressed "through a cycle." Aristotle's theory of government, our own proof of the cycle through which we have gone since before the fall of Rome; Darwin's theory of evolution and now mental evolution, all go to prove the same thing.

Of course the psychological treatment of mental evolution is entirely too broad to consider fully, so we have to limit it to one branch. This will be the development of language or articulate speech where seems to be, what some consider, the impassable bridge between man and beast. To begin with we will have to distinguish six different kinds of language. First, sounds which are neither articulate or rational, as cries of pain, etc.; second, sounds which are articular but not rational, as talk of parrots, or of certain idiots; third, sounds which are rational but not articulate, ejaculations by which we sometimes express assent to, or dissent from, given propositions; fourth, sounds which are both rational and articulate, constituting true speech; fifth, gestures which do not answer to ratioanal conceptions but are merely the manifestations of emotions and feelings; sixth, gestures which do answer to rational conceptions and are therefore external but natural manifestations of emotions and feelings.

Signs are really the first phase of language, and these are found to a highly developed degree in all animals, even in the lowest forms. When we consider the high degree to which ants carry the principle of co-operation, it is very evident that they must have some means of intercommunication.

Lastly as a proof that the more intelligent of the lower animals admit of being taught the use of signs of the most conventional character can be proven by some recent experiments by Sir John Lubbock. These experiments consisted in writing on separate cards such words as "bone," "water,' "out," "pet me," etc., and teaching the dog to bring the card bearing the word expressive of his wants at the time of bringing it. So an association of ideas was established between the appearance of a certain number and form of written signs and the meaning which they severally betokened. Sir John Lubbock found that his dog learned the correct use of those signs. Of course, it is absurd to suppose that the dog could read the letters, but then these experiments are of great interest in showing that it falls within the mental capacity of the more intelligent animals to appreciate the use of signs so conventional as those which constitute a stage of writing above the drawing of pictures and below the employment of an alphabet. Now it has been clearly proven that animals present the germ of the sign-making faculty. As it is the purpose to estimate the probability of the human language having arisen by way of continuous development in this germ, a general survey brings us to the conclusion that one and two are on a psychological level in man and animals; three is also especially in its branch; case four is to a large extent psychologically equivalent in man and animals, and difference lies in the fact that the higher psychical man is more rich in ideas.

The least conventional of the systems is the language of tone and gesture. Take the infant to begin with; we know that the wishes and emotions of very young children are conveyed in a small number of sounds but in a great variety of gestures and facial expressions. A child's gestures are intelligent long in advance of its speech, although it is being continually taught in the latter and not in former. The Indian pantomime is not merely capable of expressing a few simple and ordinary notions, but this serves as a fair substitute for a scanty vocabulary. In the case of the deaf mute who through signs and gestures told how he, when a boy, went to a melon field and there cut a slice off a ripe melon. A man made his appearance on horseback, entered the patch on foot, found the melon cut and detecting the thief, threw the melon towards him, hitting him on the back, whereupon he ran away crying. Now all this was told by the gesture and sign language, so one can readily see to what degree sign language can be developed. No one denies the fact that this is present in the beast, do they?

So summing up we may say that gesture language is the most natural or immediate mode of giving expression to the logic of recepts. Here we must digress a little in order to explain the word recept. Mr. Romanes divides ideation into three large groups, ideas perceived; perceptions; ideas received or recepts and ideas conceived or conceptions. The points to which to draw special attention in this gesture language are the absence of the copula, and of many other "parts of speech". The order in which ideas are expressed, pictorial devices by which the ideas are presented in as concrete a form as possible, and the fact that no ideas of any high abstraction are ever expressed at all.

Next to be considered is articualtion, which we will present under four headings for the sake of clearness: first articulation by way of meaningless imitation, second meaningless articulation by the way of spontaneous exercise of the organs of speech, third understanding of the signification of articulate sounds or words, and fourth articulation with an intentional attribution of the meaning understood as attaching to the words. Meaningless imitation, as we all know without being offered proof, occurs in talking birds;

young children, not unfrequently in savages, in idiots and in the mentally deranged. The second case is also recognized as a psychological fact both in animals and young infants. Now the third point, that is the understanding of articulate speech, becomes a more important consideration. Words are coined expressly for the use of concepts, or ideas conceived. The understanding of words imply a higher development of the sign making faculty than does the understanding of a tone or gesture. Higher animals unquestionably understand the meaning of words; idiots too low in the scale to speak are in the same position, and infants long before they begin to talk learn the signification of articulate sound. The understanding of words is a much higher grade of mental evolution than the understanding of tones.

The fourth point is easily proven by the fact of the talking birds, by correctly using proper names, noun substantives, adjectives, verbs and appropriate phrases, although they do so by association alone or without appreciation of structure. On this subject we have some odd illustrations of children who have formed languages of their own of queer articulation. They are German but of English birth and speak neither the mother tongue nor the English. These children understand each other and no one else.

Now from the "Articulation" stage we will pass on to the relation which tone and gesture bear to words. Words like gestures are signs of thought and feelings but they are more pure signs. Colonel Malleny, though, says that gesture language "when highly cultivated its rapidity on familiar subjects exceeds that of speech and approaches that of thought (conceptual idea) itself. So it is easily shown how receptual ideas may be so highly developed as to prove that conceptual idea is merely a higher development or an evolution of receptual ideas. Tones and gestures were first used but when words were developed it was merely a case of "survival of the fittest" or analogous to the process by which iron has become the exclusive material of swords and gold and silver for money. Words are economical, therefore they have come to be used. Psychologically gesture-language is not able to convey ideas of any high degree of abstraction. That the brute is not able to articulate cannot be ascribed to anything but an anatomical condition as distinguished from psychological conditions; for not only are the higher monkeys much more intelligent than talking birds but are more imitative of human gestures. Now, then, seeing that the monkey uses its voice more freely than other animals in the way of intentionally expressive intonation; that all higher animals make use of gesture signs; that denotative words are nothing more than vocal gestures, that psychologically the interval between simple gesticulation and denotative articulation in the case of talking birds, infants and idiots. Now the only thing upon which opponents of evolution may take their stand is the faculty of speech.

In the first place we must understand that "Speech" is a particular kind of sign making. Now the distinctive peculiarity of this sign making consists in predication or the using of signs as movable types for the purpose of making propositions. It does not signify whether or no the signs thus used are words. The distinction resides in the intellectual powers not in the symbols thereof. So a man means, it doesn't matter by what signs he expresses his meaning, the distinction between him and the brute consists in his being able to mean a proposition. This act is called Judgment, and now have we come to the point where man and beast mentally differ, but this is not generic but rather a difference in degree. If a brute could think "is" brute and man would be brothers. Here is the point where instinct ends and reason begins. Now we must come to the transition. Man is endowed with self-consciousness, but there is a time when the child is not conscious of self, this is the time when the child has real perceptions. Now it is in this state that we can draw our most satisfactory conclusions between man and beast and show how speech has been evolved. The child has as yet only perceptual or pre-conceptual ideas; the beast also receptual ideas as has been proven by many examples. In the state that the child is now in does he not use gesture or sign language, articulation, etc., but not as yet speech that comes as a later result possibly caused as much by environment as anything. The conceptual brings in the Judgment which we can neither prove nor disprove that the beast is possessor of. All sciences seem to be tending toward the proof of this broad question of evolution but as yet it has not been entirely accepted by the whole scientific world but no doubt soon will be.

Gertrude Wayne, '11.

"THE SONGS OF VAGABONDIA."

To really appreciate "The Songs of Vagabondia" you must take them with you on a long country walk. You are resting on the grass beside the road, which winds on out of sight. All around you is life and space. Everything is green and seems to be growing before your very eyes. You have the same spirit in you that made the puppy you passed, race up and down the road, and the birds sing merrily. Now is the time for Bliss Carmen's "Spring Song."

Make me over, Mother April,
When the sap begins to stir!
When thy flowery hand delivers
All the mountain-prisoned rivers,
And thy great heart beats and quivers
To revive the days that were.
Make me over, Mother April,
When the sap begins to stir!"

The poems are full of the out of doors. They breathe the spirit of it.

"Now the joys of the road are chiefly these:
A crimson touch on the hard wood trees;
A vagrants morning wide and blue,
In early fall when the winds walk too;
A shadowy highway cool and brown,
Alluring up and enticing down
From rippled water to dappled swamp,
From purple glory to scarlet pomp."

"Spray salt gusts of ocean blow
From the rocky headlands;
Overhead the wild geese fly,
Honking on the autumn sky;
Black sinister flocks of crows
Settle on the dead lands."

This feeling for the out of doors and Vagabondia is at the basis of Bliss Carmen's and Richard Hovey's philosophy. To them life is Vagabondia, and in that spirit they view it. They frankly enjoy the experiences that come and meet them half way.

There is no affectation in their view point. They are not afraid. Friendship is comradeship in the journey. This thought is often expressed.

"Three of us to march abreast
Down the hills of morrow!
With a clean heart and a few
Friends to clinch the spirit to!—
Leave the gods to rule the rest,
And good by sorrow.'

Again

"You to the left and I to the right,
For the way of men must sever,
And it well may be for a day and a night,
And it well may be forever!
But whether we live or whether we die
(For the end is past our knowing),
Here's two frank hearts and the open sky
Be a fair or an ill wind blowing!
Here's luck
In the teeth of all winds blowing."

This philosophy enables these poets to see even themselves in a true light. Their prise aof Shakespeare and Browning and other great men is hearty and sincere. Turning to his own verse, Bliss Carmen says, with a keen humor not often turned on one's self,

I can see myself, O Burgess, half a century from now
Laid to rest among the ghostly, like a broken toy somehow;
All my lovely songs and ballads vanished with your Purple Cow.

It naturally follows that they had little respect for the hypocracies of other people. Turn to "The Sceptic",

"Said Gross, 'What is that noise
That startles and destroys
Our blessed summer brooding when we're tired?
'That's folks a-praising God,'
Said the tough old cynic clod;
'They do it every Sunday
They'll be all right on Monday;
It's just a little habit they've acquired'."

And lest you should think these men flippant let me quote once more, this time from the closing poem written by Bliss Carmen and Richard Hovey together.

"We have cast in our lot with Truth;
We will not flinch nor stay the hand,
Till on the last skyline of youth
We look down on his promised land.

We put from port without a fear,
For freedom on this Spanish Main;
And the great wind that bore us here
Will drive our galleys home again.

If not we can lie down and die,
Content to perish with our peers,
So one more rood we gained thereby
For Love's Dominion through the years."

In the three little volumes that compose the verses, many subjects are treated, each individually. Now you come across a delicate little love lyric, or a stirring ballad that reminds you of Kipling. Many places are described and often a single object like a flower is the subject; sometimes a word seems to be hurled on the paper, as when he begins

"I think it must be spring. I feel
All broken up and thawed.
I'm sick of everybody's 'wheel';
I'm sick of being jawed."

The metres are as varied as the subjects. They are often musical and help to express the spirit of the poem by their rhythm. Or often they are rough and unpolished and perhaps in that very way express the thought.

Yet with all the different subjects and their individuality of treatment, the spirit which I have described runs through all. They are not great works of art nor do they give any very new ideas. Yet they are honest and healthy and human and in expressing the thoughts which may have come to us too, they are more satisfying to certain moods than great and wonderful poetry.

Mary D. Lindsay.

SKETCHES

"A COUNTRY SALE.'

There was great curiosity among the summer boarders in the little Ohio town about the country sale. "A real country sale would be an experience," we said. And it was an "experience," but not such as we had expected.

We saw there an old man of ninety years looking on mutely, appealingly, as the coarse-witted auctioneer tried to dispose of the antiquated furniture, dishes and books which had made up home. It seemed that but a week before Betsy, his wife, had died and he, broken hearted and too old to face the world alone, had decided to get what he could from the poor furnishings—enough to buy a marker for her who had been so dear. The bids were ridiculously low—more so than usual, it seemed. In early years these prosaic farmers of the country side had had no use for the pair of dreamers who found more pleasure in admiring the landscape than in tilling the soil. And when in their old age the county had had to come to the rescue with a monthly pension, the thrifty neighbors had ostracised "that shiftless Nathe and his wife" completely.

Finally the last thing was sold, "old Nathe" with the proceeds of the sale—$17.23—in his pocket hobbled slowly down the walk to the county farm buggy and with one last look drove away never to return. As the sun set over the beautiful vale that afternoon our voices were hushed—we had seen one of the tragedies of life—the vale itself had become a veritable "valley of the shadow."

Rachel D. McQuiston, '11.

WHAT A CITY BABE MISSES.

There are perhaps five million human machines in New York City. This includes the children; for it would be difficult to state at exactly how early a stage in their infancy the babies are wound up. One is almost justified in believing that they are born "wound up".

Do not talk of the barbarism of the savages. It is humane and beautiful when contrasted with the outrages of civilization. In this great city three babes out of every four open their eyes upon bleak outer or inner walls, and their ears upon the cobble stone rattle and the steel rail buzz. Little eyes that should look right from mother love straight out into universal nature love!

I pity the baby that is wakened by the hum of the city in place of the call of the lark. I pity the baby that is accompanied to sleep by the whirr of wheels in place of the lullaby of leaves. Their little faces tell a story that no one cares to read. Click! Click! go their tiny bodies. Click! Click! go their tiny minds. Click! Click! go their tiny souls. "Very good machines," you assure me. "Very good." I gravely acknowledge, "but machines."

What one misses in them is life: life that nods its head as carelessly burden-free as the dandelion; life that throws forth its fragrance with as happy prodigality as the southern jessamine; life that surrenders itself in death with as gallant courtesy as some monarch oak yields up its all.

What one misses in their city is kinship: the kinship of the daily nod, and the smile, and the handclasp; the kinship which breeds humaneness and begets sympathy and tolerance; the kinship that finds its song in the mirth of true humor, not that humor of mind that we call wit but the humor of the heart which is no more to be likened to wit than the dimple is to be explained by the frown; the kinship that rests in a pervasive human sense of humor better than religion itself in its mantle of charity, the true humor that in its charity is a religion.

What the babe misses (and what one misses in the babe) are the hills high protective and secure; the hills whose vales are as gardens of peace and love; the hills whose garments are as robes of state to an infant mind and heart; the hills that stand as a promise and a symbol between you and their purple mystery, which some one has feebly named the other side of them.

M. L. C.

"WORDS, IDLE WORDS!"

I never realized how many unnecessary words I use until I went into a Chinese laundry the other day with some work I wanted done. Had I been in an American shop, I would probably have said,

"I have here some collars that I wish to have laundered. I am in a great hurry for them and want them just as soon as I can possibly have them. Now, can you promise them to me the last of the week, without fail?"

I should have considered that much a definite and concise statement of my wishes. As it was, I handed the package to the Chinaman.

"When?" said I.

He opened the package and examined the contents. "Fliday," he answered.

"Sure?" I asked.

He nodded; and I left.

Association with those who speak a foreign tongue may give us some pointers as to the value of brevity. L. M., '13.

FULFILLMENT OF DREAMS.

Said Mary when I'm six years old
To school I'm going to go,
And even when it's very cold
I'll go in spite of snow.

"I'll like it more each year" she cried
"Than Christmas or ice cream";
But I'm afraid she lied, she lied
Or cared not for ice cream.

So soon to school up in the dell
Dear Mary gladly went,
Nor could a mortal ever tell
The joy of this event.

But what were Mary's feelings when
To college she must go?
Ha! Ha! my lady stormed and raged,
And brother cried, "I told you so."

Gertude Wayne, '11.

THE SOROSIS
Published Monthly by the Students of
Pennsylvania College for **Women.**

Ethel Tassey, '10 .... Editor-in-Chief
Elma McKibben, '10 .... Business Manager
Minerva Hamilton, '11 .... Literary Editor
Elvira Estep, '12 .... College Notes
Calla Stahlman, '12 .... Personals
Marguerite Frey, '13 .... Exchanges
Gertrude Wayne, '11 .... Assistant Business Manager

Subscriptions to the Sorosis, 75 cents per year. Single copies, 10c.
Address all business communications to the Business Manager.
Entered in the Postoffice at Pittsburg, Pa., as second-class matter.

A HAPPY AND PROSPEROUS NEW YEAR.

Of course we have all returned from our vacation with a beautifully framed set of "Resolutions", every one of which is to be kept absolutely to the letter. Some of these new leaves have been turned over with reference to our school life; chapel is to be attended regularly, classes are never more to be cut, and lessons shall most religiously be prepared. In fact life in general will be as near perfect as human agency can make it and will move along as beautiful and tranquil as a woodland stream.

'Tis ever thus! 'Tis also a fact that these most laudable resolutions are invariably completely smashed. Not that it is a lack of desire or will to keep them, but the mere contrariness of human nature that opposes any fixed determination to turn aside from the easiest course.

But without taking the trouble to do any resolving, it might be a good idea and might really be effective if each one could feel an individual responsibility in regard to the work and institutions of the College, to have respect for the Rules of Student Government and last but not least to give hearty support and cooperation to the Sorosis.

The Sorosis heartily congratulates Miss Florence Wilson as the winner of the prize in the Short Story Contest. The story itself is humorous, ingenious and undoubtedly true to life. It is to be hoped that success on this occasion will encourage Miss Wilson to continue work along this line. All the stories entered were exceptionaly good so that it was not a simple matter for the judges to render a decision. They really found three prize stories, but since there could only be one "First Prize" Honorable Mention was awarded "The Voice of a Nation" by Minerva Hamilton, '11, and "The Soul of a Violin" by Frances Cameron '11. The Sorosis greatly appreciates the active interest shown in the contest and wishes to thank especially Miss Coolidge and Mr. Putnam, who kindly consented to act as judges; and Miss Lilla Greene '08, who originated the Sorosis Contests and has offered the Prize for the last two years.

ALUMNAE.

Announcement has been made of the marriage of Miss Florence Van Wagener '05 to Mr. Rutledge Shaw, January twenty-fifth.

Mrs. Walter Dann entertained the Decade Club II at her home in Wilkinsburg, January fourteenth.

Miss Irma Beard, '09, has accepted a position as teacher of Latin and Algebra in the High School at Stoneboro, Pa.

Miss Edna McKee was the guest of Mrs. Armstrong at dinner Thursday evening, January twentieth.

Miss Gladwin Coburn, '09' is assisting Miss Hogue in the laboratory.

Miss Edith Gray entertained at cards at her home in Linden Avenue during the Christmas holidays. A number of P. C. W. alumnae were among those present.

At a tea given by Miss Harriet Pew of Grove City announcement was made of the engagement of her sister, Miss Elizabeth Pew, '05' to Mr. Ambrose Harvey Bell of Pittsburgh.

At a recent meeting of the Alumnae Association, the members were greatly pleased to learn that one thousand dollars had been raised with which to furnish the kitchen and dining rooms of South Hall.

The outside World seems to appreciate the Alumnae of P. C. W. On Christmas day Miss Coulter, '09' received a box of candy from the head of her school; underneath the candy was a gold watch in token of appreciation of her services.

COLLEGE NOTES.

The Christmas dance was a great success in every way. The living room and reception rooms were decorated with Christmas flowers and little Christmas trees, and the fireplace was banked with green and poinsettia. South Hall is an ideal place for a dance.

The College enjoyed the delightful lecture given by Dr. Kelso, President of the Western Theological Seminary, on Wednesday morning, January twelfth. His subject was, "Recent Finds in Bible Lands."

The Sophomores gave a very pretty little Japanese Operetta entitled "Princess Chrysanthemum", on Friday evening, January fourteenth. Those who took part in the production were:

Princess Chrysanthemum—The Emperor's Daughter		Martha Sands
To-To		Gladwin Coburn
Yum-Yum	Maidens attendant on Princess	Mary Gray
Du-du		Daisy Sharp
Tu-lip		Elvira Estep
Fairy Moonbeam—The Princess's Good Genius		Florence Bickel
Prince So-Tru	In love with Princess	Helen Grooms
Prince So-Sli		Martha Kim
Top-Not—The Court Chamberlain		Lillie Lindsay

Saucer-Eyes—The Wizard Cat..................Edith Chaddock
Sprites of the Night, Courtiers, Populace, Attendants, Fairies, etc.

Scene I—The Emperor's Garden.

Scene II—The Cave of Inky Night.

Scene III—Same as Scene I.

The annual Christmas dinner, Thursday evening, December sixteenth, heralded the Holiday Season for the members of the Household. The dining room of Berry Hall presented a very pretty scene with its Christmas decorations. Each table was decorated by a special committee according to its original ideas. Santa Claus was present with his sleigh and reindeer, Christmas trees, poinsettia, and even a chimney were in evidence. Each person received a gift selected with a view to her particular hobby. At the close of the dinner Christmas carols and old folk songs were sung.

Mrs. Catherine Oliver McCoy gave us a most interesting talk, "The Confessions of a Literary Pilgrim," Wednesday morning, January nineteenth, in Assembly Hall. Her interpretation of the Scotch dialect was delightful.

French and German tables have been arranged for in the dining room of Berry Hall at which the students and Faculty have an opportunity of conversing at least once a week in a foreign tongue. Before they were undertaken a few wise suggestions were made in regard to them: "Cultivate an intelligent look." "Seem to be intensely interested." "When you can't finish a German sentence end it up with 'doch'." In French "Oui, Oui" with a nod and a smile or 'b'ien" will help wonderfully. So far these tables have proved quite a success. If everyone could not speak fluently, at least they seemed to have no difficulty in eating and laughing.

Tuesday afternoon, January eighteenth, the Faculty entertained in honor of Mr. and Mrs. Putnam. A few outside guests were invited.

The new Rest Room of South Hall is occupied at last. Many have congratulated Miss Blakeslee on being the first occupant, but just now the patient doesn't seem to appreciate the fancy pin cushion and the real nurse with a uniform.

Saturday, January twenty-ninth, the Association of Collegiate Alumnae will entertain the girls of the third and fourth year classes of preparatory and high schools. It is the object of this association to interest girls in a college education. In Dilworth Hall stereopticon views will be shown of scenes and festivities of all the large colleges for women, including our own. Later the guests will make a tour of inspection of our buildings under the guidance of the college girls.

PERSONALS.

Misses Florence Bickel, Mary Gray, Martha Sands, May Hardy, Helen Blair, and Margaret Corbett are living at South Hall during the winter months.

Miss Amelia Horst entertained at her home in North Side, in honor of Miss Anna Larimer, her house guest, December thirty-first.

A number of the Glee and Mandolin Club girls attended the Annual Concert given by Carnegie Technical Glee and Mandolin Clubs, Wednesday night, January nineteenth, at Carnegie Music Hall.

Who started the "swirl craze" in South Hall? It takes close scrutiny to recognize one's friends.

Miss S. (translating German)—Fallsucht—falling sickness—dropsy.

No story-telling fest is complete without Miss T.'s characteristic remark: "Oh, I know a joke but I can't remember it."

Miss MacFarland has accepted the position of matron of South Hall. Mrs. Reynolds resigned the position during the holidays.

Announcements have been received of the marriage of Mr. George W. Putnam to Miss Edith Clarke of Boston, December twenty-eight. Mr. and Mrs. Putnam will be at home to their friends at 5502 Kentucky Avenue, after February first.

Sincerest sympathy is extended to Miss Kerst who has been called to her home at Greenville, Ohio, on account of the death of her father.

Since the death of her brother Miss Green has been obliged to give up teaching and will leave for her home at Granville, Ohio, Friday, January twenty-eighth.

MUSIC NOTES.

The Mandolin Club has been reorganized with a number of new members. Miss Hebrank of Wilkinsburg has been chosen a director of the club. Rehearsals are being held every week; they show rapid progress and promise great success for the future.

The Japanese Operetta given by the Sophomores was a new departure in the College Dramatics. This was the first attempt at Comic Opera and the work of the soloists and chorus in the numerous musical selections was a delightful surprise. The class is justly proud of its musical ability.

A recital of Early Music, chiefly seventeenth century music, was given by T. Carl Whitmir, pianist, assisted by Miss Pauline Harrington, contralto, Friday evening, January 21, 1910, in Assembly Hall. Selections were given from Bull, Byrd, Loelly, Couperin, Galuppi, Bach, Krebs; also Shakespearian songs, from Ballet, Johnson, Vernon, and Old Welsh, Scotch and Irish Songs. Mr. Whitmir's interpretation is splendid, and Miss Harrington is a pleasing soloist.

The Glee Club is working on plans for a number of affairs in the future.

EXCHANGES.

The Washington-Jeffersonian excels especially in its editorial department. An editorial in the January issue deserves high commendation for the spirit with which it upholds the Honor System.

In the Night of the Comets.

Dread no longer Halley's
Comet,
Hide not in dark valleys
From it;
Noxious gas? A guess or
Howler,
Says the great Professor
Fowler;
'Tis a harmless, ghostly
Skittish
Traveller who's mostly
British;
More of Brock than Pain 'twill
Bring us,
Halo as of saint will
Fling us;
Fifteen million miles of
"Skirting,"
Not a thought these isles of
Hurting,
Like a fairy chain of
Ballets
Sweeps that gold lace train of
Halley's,
Heavenly bunch of flora,
Human
As a peacock, or a
Woman!

—London Chronicle.

he Christmas Exchanges were very attractive and ht holiday stories.

an named his coachman Procrastination, because he

.

Now I lay me down to rest
For tomorrow is an awful test;
If I should die before I wake,
Thank heaven, I'll have no test to take.

Why They Giggled.

"Why girls giggle" has been made the subject of many inquiries. The ultimate reason is not yet known, but investigators hope for a solution some time. Meanwhile, the following, from the New York Evening Sun, may throw some light upon the mystery. Two young ladies were standing in front of the window of a dry-goods store. "Tee-hee-hee!" giggled the first young lady. "Tee-hee-hee!" giggled the second young lady. "What on earth are you laughing at?"

"Tee-hee-hee!" giggled the first. "It's that—O dear!—it's that man—tee-hee-hee!—behind the ribbon counter—Grrh!—in here! Oh, tee-hee-hee! Oh, tee-hee-hee!"

"Oh, tee-hee-hee! What's he— Oh, tee-hee-hee! What's he been doing now?"

"It's— Oh, tee-hee-hee! It's— Oh, tee-hee-hee!—it's the way he says good morning. O dear, O dear, O dear, I just know I shall die!"

And as the fear of imminent doom laid hold of her she snorted into her handkerchief with such a merry emphasis that they both nearly died, but after a terrible struggle each one succeeded in straightening her face, and they entered the store and made for the ribbon counter as solemn as any judges, but somewhat more red in the face.

"Grrrrrh!" choked the first young lady.

"Grrrrrh!" choked the second young lady.

The ribbon clerk had the pale voice and the feeble face of a man grown gray in the service of pleasing the ladies, but aside from that he was not quite so productive of merriment as the Pyramids.

"Grrrrrh!" choked the first young lady.

"Grrrrrh!" choked the second young lady.

"Tee-hee-hee!" exploded the first young lady.

"Tee-hee-hee!" exploded the second young lady.

And turning suddenly away the two little madams shook their shoulders as if with the ague, and every time either one stole a glance at the other there were such paroxysms of mirth as never were before on land or sea.

"I want—" said the first young lady, turning round at last.

"Oh, tee-hee-hee!" burst out the second young lady.

"Oh, tee-hee-hee!" burst out the first. "I—I want—"

"Oh, tee-hee-hee!" gasped the other. "Oh-oh-oh, tee-hee-hee!"

"I want," began the first young lady, "half a yard of—"

"Grrrrrh!" snorted the second young lady.

"Grrrrrh!" snorted the first.

"Oh, tee-hee-hee!" giggled the second young lady, with vigor refreshed.

"Oh, tee-hee-hee!" giggled the first.

And as they weakly helped each other from the store, their handkerchiefs crushed to their faces, tottering, exploding, snorting, and weaving the richest designs of mirth with their shoulders and the backs of their heads, an old philosopher looked over from across the street and sadly said to himself:

"I see I was wrong, for some of them **have** a sense of humor, after all."

Studious—"If I buy a pony will it save half my studying?"

Clerk—"Yes.'

Studious—"Gimme two!"—Ex.

Class Stones.

Freshman—Emerald.
Sophomore—Blarney Stone.
Junior—Grindstone.
Senior—Tombstone.—Ex.

"Little grains of humor,
Little bits of bluff
Make the little Freshmen,
Think they're just the stuff."
—Ex.

POTTERY
Hamilton & Clark Co.
208 OLIVER AVENUE
NEW LOCATION
CHINA
GLASS

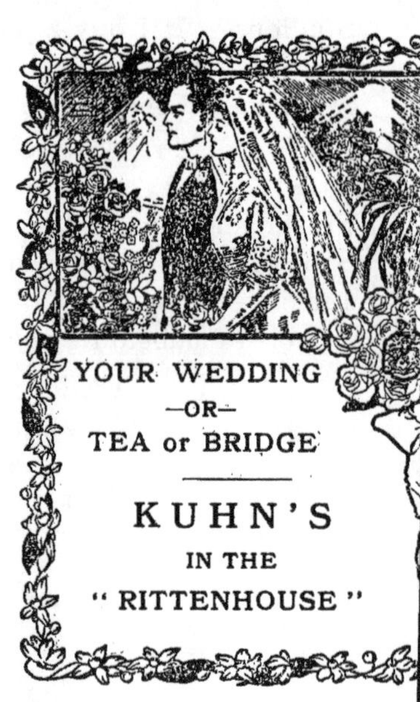
YOUR WEDDING
—OR—
TEA or BRIDGE
KUHN'S
IN THE
"RITTENHOUSE"

THE SOROSIS

VOL. XVI FEBRUARY, 1910 No. 4

OMAR KAYYAM AND RABBI BEN EZRA.

At the time that Fitzgerald's translation of the Rubaiyat of Omar Kayyam was published, Browning was living in Italy. He may have obtained the book from Rossetti to whom Swinburn had sent a copy. The Rabbi Ben Ezra might very easily have been written as an answer to the Rubaiyat.

The poems can be studied very well together, being directly opposite in ethical teaching, each heightening and intensifying the other. The teaching of Rabbi Ben Ezra is based upon hope in the future,—that of Omar Kayyam upon enjoyment of the present.

Omar Kayyam sees neither into the past nor into the future. The whole of the Rubaiyat points out that life should be enjoyed while it lasts; the individual is of no particular consequence in the general scheme of things; the flesh is at least as immortal as the spirit; heaven and hell lie within the individual, heaven, the fulfillment of desires, hell, the "shadow of the soul on fire." Therefore, to struggle toward the fulfillment of desire is to enjoy a paradise while still living. We have no responsibility for the future, pleasure is the only aim of life.

> "Ah, make the most of what we may yet spend,
> Before we, too, into the Dust descend;
> Dust into Dust, and under Dust to lie,
> Sans Wine, sans Song, sans Singer, and—sans End!"

Browning holds that life is a preparation for the future, that pleasure is the least important of aims.

"Poor vaunt of life indeed,
Were man but formed to feed
On joy, to solely seek and find and feast;
Such feasting ended, then
As sure an end to men;
Irks care the cropful bird? Frets doubt the maw crammed beast?"

According to Browning failure is often real success—

"Learn, nor account the pang; dare, never grudge the throe!
What I aspired to be,
And was not, comforts me:
A brute I might have been, but would not sink in the scale."

On the other hand, Omar Kayyam thinks that even success is failure; work and struggle are worth nothing.

"The worldly hope men set their hearts upon
Turns ashes,—or it prospers; and anon,
Like snow upon the Desert's dusty face,
Lighting a little hour or two—was gone."

To Browning the flesh is merely the vessel that contains the soul, it has no immortality, no consciousness after death. Omar Kayyam is sure that the flesh, at least, is eternal, and that every drop of wine that falls upon the earth rejoices some clod that once was man. But authors grant that the soul is of the same essence as God. Browning thinks that after a life spent in struggle for the highest and purest things, man dies having in his soul at last some spark of God; he calls such a soul, "a god but in the germ". Omar Kayyam recognizes no superiority in the Divine Spirit over his own soul, aside from His power. God is no wiser, no better than man.

"O thou, who man of baser earth didst make
And e'en with Paradise devised the snake:
For all the Sin wherewith the Face of Man
Is blackened—Man's Forgiveness give—and take!"

To Browning failure, struggle, rebuffs, adversity, are all for the development of the soul, and its refinement for the next life. Omar Kayyam does not admit that the soul is more advanced in development after a long life of struggle, but that it is the same in the end as at the beginning. He himself has passed through a long period of questioning and searching—it brings him to nothing. He attains neither faith in God, nor love for Him. Browning has both. Omar Kayyam comes out of his study as wise as he entered upon it,—he finds a mystery which there is nothing within him to solve. Browning holds his work as preparation for a greater, better life to come. Omar Kayyam comes to the conclusion in that there is neither future nor past, only a present that must be made the most of. Browning withdraws his hopes and aims from this life to place them in the next.

Both philosophers use the simile of the Potter moulding the clay. Browning trusts in the wisdom and love of the Potter, he is sure that He will smooth out the blemishes in the vessel when the proper time comes.

"So take and use thy work:
Amend what flaws may lurk,
What strain o' the stuff, what warpings past the aim!
My times be in thy hand!
Perfect the cup as planned!
Let age approve of youth, and death complete the same!"

Omar Kayyam blames the Potter for the blemishes in the cup; he has no faith in the ultimate wholeness of the vessel. He thinks he could have done God's work better than He Himself has done it.

"Ah, Love! could you and I with Him conspire
To grasp this sorry scheme of things entire,
Would not we shatter it to bits—and then
Re-mould it nearer to the Heart's Desire."

Browning looks forward to death as to a door opened into a finer, higher life. Omar Kayyam thinks that he will have accomplished enough if he does not shrink from Death. His death is of no consequence anyhow, so why worry about it, why not make the most of life while it lasts?

Omar Kayyam's is the stern pagan philosophy, Rabbi Ben Ezra is nearer the Christian, in his hope and faith. Yet the cheerfulness of Omar's pessimism leaves a happier feeling in the reader, than the sombre, struggling optimism of the Rabbi.

Irma Diescher, '11.

THE VOICE OF A NATION.

(Honorable Mention in the Short Story Contest.)

The minister and the maltese cat sat dozing before the study fire. The man lay back in his arm-chair, almost completely enveloped in a bright, pink comforter, traced with trailing vines of vivid green, one tendril of which rippled gracefully from the minister's chin to the tips of the minister's broad carpet-slippers, which peeped up from a low foot-stool before the blaze. His hair was as white as the January snows without and his bald head had the same wind-swept appearance as the low hills visible through the windows. A sudden gust of wind rattled the shutters with such unusual vigor that the maltese cat raised its head quickly and crept nearer to the warmth of the grate, while the minister burst into a fit of coughing which awakened him somewhat rudely from his slumbers.

With a start he seized his pen anew and turned his attention to the manuscript before him. Where was he? Oh yes; the free press as an organ of truth—the voice of a nation—the voice of truth. Yes, to be sure. The free press was a wonderful thing, the mighty voice of a mighty people—well— His pen began a new paragraph and continued its scratching progress, interrupted by frequent vigorous taps which signified emphatic punctuation. At last it reached the climax of the sermon and paused, suspended in air, while its owner meditated.

The minister looked out with evident anxiety upon shivering maples and wind-blown patches of snow. Through the lace work of trees he saw the village lying still and cold beneath; its low houses huddled closely together, with one lone church spire rising slender and grey from their midst. It was cold,—cold. He shivered and turned with relief to the glowing, crackling blaze. No, he could not possibly attend church tomorrow, and no word had been received from the city. He glanced uneasily at the shelf above the fire-place. Four o'clock! What if no one could be found to fill his pulpit?

"Matilda, Matilda!" he called in hoarse tones. "Can you co—" the sentence ended in a cough.

The door was opened gently by a little, old lady with snowy hair drawn back in tight, little crimps above a patient, sweet face. She hurried across the room and drew the pink comforter closer about her husband's throat.

"Now there, do keep that closer about you, and don't worry about getting some one to take your place tomorrow. No, Dr. James has not called up yet, but, even if he can't find any one," she continued cheerfully. "There's Deacon Potter. You're writing it all out and he might read it. He'll enjoy reading it, I do believe, even more than hearing it—Oh no, I don't mean he would not enjoy and appreciate your sermon, but you know how eager he is to seize every opportunity to 'speechify'."

The minister frowned. "No," emphatically. "Deacon Potter would make a mess of it. He would weaken all my strong points and emphasize all the minor ones. If Dr. James can find no one, I'm afraid Chester will have to go without a sermon for once, unless," he continued jestingly, "You can read it for me." He laughed.

His wife stared blankly for a minute, rather dazed by such a suggestion. She, a woman, an old woman, fill her husband's place and preach his sermon to all those people? But then why should she not? She often led missionary meetings and, as president of the Emerson Club, was frequently called upon to address that society. Why should she be afraid? With a sudden smile of determination she patted the minister on the shoulder.

"Why couldn't I?" she asked. "Hugh, I will. But oh"—she hesitated, "all those people. Perhaps Dr. James will find some one and if he does not I will."

And so she did. Late that night came a telephone message that Dr. James was unable to secure a substitute for the pulpit of Chester church. The minister forthwith completed his manuscript and proceeded to test his wife's powers of oratory. Twice, elevated upon a landing in the hall stairway, she read the lengthy discourse through, interrupted by occasional suggestions from her audience, the minister, the pink comforter, and the Maltese cat.

"Don't forget to give due emphasis to that point, Matilda. Pause before 'The voice of a nation.' Now suppose you try again; you read it very well."

The next day dawned crisp, but sparkling and sunshiny. A biting wind blew in penetrating blasts from the north. In spite of cold and snow, however, the congregation at Chester was large that day, and many were the tremblings and quakings felt by the timid, little old lady behind the high reading desk. How she managed it she never knew but she did, finally, reach the end of that seemingly unending sermon, through the free press and all the rest of it. Church over, she hurried home to be consoled by the minister, the comforter, and the Maltese cat.

* * * * * * * * * * *

The winter sunlight shown brightly in upon the luncheon table, where the minister sat at one end, reading Monday's "Herald," while his wife busied herself with the rosebud china at the other. No sound disturbed the quiet save the subdued tinkle of china and silver, and the rattle of paper as the minister turned a page. Suddenly, a puzzled expression crept into his countenance, followed by amazement, then anger.

"What?" he almost shouted.

His wife popped out of her chair with a start.

"The—the—, read that,' he gasped, holding out the paper.

His wife did so in nervous wonder. There in great headlines she read:

"Woman suddenly Wins Great Fame as Preacher.

With Husband on Deathbed Parson's brave Wife fills Pulpit and Preaches Great Sermon."

Then followed a humorous, grossly exaggerated account of the "fiery eloquence of a middle-aged lady moving audience to tears." It did not hesitate to mention her name.

The papers fell rattling to the floor, and the poor little, white-haired lady gazed back at her husband, an expression of incredulous mazament in her face.

"They wrote that—about—me?" she queried, a hurt look creeping into her eyes, "Oh, how could they?"

Her husband raged up and down the room with such vehemence that the Maltese cat retired with discreet haste.

"The insolence! What on earth—How could such a mistake be made? It must be rectified; I shall remonstrate, immediately." He closed his lips in a firm, determined line and strode into the hall.

"Don't go out in the cold," pleaded his wife." Don't mind; it's, really it's funny," and she laughed hysterically.

But he would not be dissuaded and soon after found himself in the busy city. As he passed along crowded, bustling streets, his ears filled with the clanging of bells, the steady roar of traffic, shouts, and the treading of many feet, he found his anger cooling somewhat. The "Herald" building was buzzing like a very industrious bee-hive, and the bees themselves in the forms of porters, office boys and pert clerks bewildered the minister with their abrupt questions and brief answers. He showed the article and requested an interview with its author.

While he waited in a little side room he drew out the paper and reread the wild account of his wife's efforts, as a substitute and his anger came back, a steady, burning indignation.

The door opened and closed again with a brisk click and a young man stepped forward. He seemed to embody a part of the activity which hummed on all sides. For a minute the older man looked at the confident young man. He noted his alert inquiring countenance, his constant, nervous movements, and his ever ready note book and pencil. Slowly his rage rose to white heat.

Thrusting the paper into the face of the young man, he demanded, "Are you the young scoundrel who wrote this article?"

The reporter looked at the designated column and an appreciative grin spread over his countenance.

"Yes, I am."

"Well, sir; the lady whom you have lied about, here, whom you have ridiculed, whom you have held up to the publicity and scorn of the whole country, is my wife. What you have written here is complete untruth—lies—and I shall be glad to know what you mean by it." He looked at the other with indignation.

"So? I'm sorry. But you see this is just the kind of thing we're hunting for. The public likes it. An incident like that means money for us. Got a raise for that article." He tapped his pad nervously with his pencil.

"But the exaggeration and the use of my wife's name. You have no right to do any such thing, to publish what is untrue about any one. I'll see what the law can do about this."

The reporter only smiled tollerantly and replied:

"I'm sorry but you can't do anything. This paper can publish everything it pleases and you can't prevent it. You ought to be glad your wife got out of it so easily. It might have been a lot worse."

"Worse? How could it have been worse?"

"Oh, you know we might have gone more into detail; published her photograph for instance."

"Do you mean to say that you had the audacity, the effrontery, to photograph my wife?"

"No, no, we did not do that but we might have published any photo and the public would believe it hers. You see, you ought to be thankful—"

"Well—," the minister stopped, unable to find words, and with one wondering, amazed look at the reporter, turned slowly, opened the door and walked out.

Out upon the snowy, traffic crowded thoroughfare, he ruminated, a dazed, hopeless expression in his face. He pushed unheeding through the crowd. As he boarded a street car a grimy, tattered, little newsboy touched him on the arm and called inquiringly, beseechingly:

"Papir, mister. Herald, Tele, Press, Times?"

But the minister did not hear. This was the free press, the voice of a nation. He shook his white head sadly. Yes, he was behind the times, behind the times.

Minerva Hamilton, '11.

THE TESTING OF DIANA MALLORY.

Mrs. Humphrey Ward's "Testing of Diana Mallory" is a novel centering around political life in the country districts of England. It is full of elections, of canvassing for votes, and political intrigues. It is of about the same character and quality as the author's former novels which are well known to readers of fiction.

The plot of this novel is good, though commonplace; it could be worked up into a fascinating romance if it were handled rightly. There is plenty of action and mystery in the book, but it is spoiled by Mrs. Ward's methods of telling the story. There are too many characters, not one of whom is normal; the heroine, Diana Mallory, is a little tiresome on account of her intense sentimentality and her unnatural profoundness of thought. Of course, the novel has its villian, in the person of Alicia Drake, who is punished in the conventional manner by not securing the man she wishes for her husband. The other characters are ordinary: the obstinate mother, the doting old man who does all the match making, the careless young man who gets into scrapes, the missionary worker, the disagreeable sister; they are all there, and are all dealt with in the conventional manner.

The setting of the story is very uninteresting to one who does not care for politics. There are chapters given over entirely to politics; these chapters lengthen out the novel to an absurd size, when one considers the simplicity of the plot.

Altogether, the book is not very good nor very bad; there are no striking qualities in it. The reader becomes tired of it after two or three hundred pages, and finds no relief as he goes on with it.

Irma Diescher, '11.

AN ILLUSTRIOUS FAMILY.

In these days when so much time and energy are employed in the study of the influence of inheritance and environment, it is well for him who has a strong, and sturdy family tree. Mrs. Florence Howe Hall, who lectured here recently, is unusually fortunate in this respect. She belongs to a family which probably contains more famous members than any other in America. It is not often that so many celebrities are found in two generations. Mrs. Hall's mother, Mrs. Julia Ward Howe, who at the age of ninety years, is still active in literature and philanthropy, will always be honored by Americans as the author of "The Battle Hymn of the Republic". Mrs. Hall's father, Dr. Samuel Howe, was famous as philanthropist, statesman, and diplomat. It was he who instituted in our country the work for the blind, it was he who abolished the public examination system in our schools; and it was he who acted as surgeon in the Greek revolution and secured supplies which saved the lives of numberless destitute.

Mrs. Hall's uncle, Samuel Ward, was an intimate friend of several of our New England men of letters: Longfellow, Emerson, Holmes and others. Himself being interested in literary work, he aided Longfellow in securing publication of many of his poems.

The sister of Mrs. Hall's mother married the artist, Thomas Crawford. Her son is Marion Crawford of whose fame it is unnecessary to speak.

Mrs. Hall has two sisters: Mrs. Laura E. Richards, known as the author of "Captain January" and other delightful stories for children; and Mrs. Maude Howe Elliott who is the wife of a famous artist in Rome. It is probable that Mrs. Hall's daughter might have won a high rank as an artist had not her career been interrupted by her recent marriage.

In her lecture, "Famous People I Have Met in My Father's House," Mrs. Hall told many anecdotes about some of our great American Men of Letters; all the more interesting, because told by one to whom the men were personally known. Among those whom she mentioned were: the poet Longfellow, Prof. Agassiz, the celebrated naturalist, whose famous school Mrs. Hall attended, Charles Sumner, Emerson, and Dr. Holmes, whose "very mouth wore a talkative expression and seemed ready to begin a conversation on a minute's notice."

SKETCHES

STUDY HOUR.

"Sed vigentes animés." Oh fudge! Gertrude, shove that "dic" over please. Have to look up about every other word of this truck. "V-i-g-e-n"—what do you suppose that comes from? Say, you should have been at the dance the other night though. Had a simply grand time. Oh, yes. Quite a large crowd but very select. Some perfectly exquisite gowns. And you should have seen Margaret. Never saw such a perfect picture in my life. She had a new gown on, stunning enough to make a ghost attractive so you can imagine how she looked. She'd look like a fairy in a calico gown and in that—,and she was with the most fascinatingly, splendid man. Forget his name but he certainly was—, oh yes, "strong." I might have known it meant something like that. Just has the "s" changed to a "g". "But strong in minds and bodies whose"—. Do you know that man was about as near my ideal as I ever met, tall and dark and handsome. Yes, I was with Fred. He is such a darling of a dancer you know. Had the dreamiest dream of a waltz with him.

"Strong in bodies and"—. I did read that. Oh yes, I left off with "robora." What does that mean? Red? Isn't there a word something like that that means red? Don't see the connection tho'. Oh my dear! You should see Jane Allen in her new red suit. If it isn't enough to have melted the Laurentian glacier. You know her complexion is terribly florid and that red dress—oh my! Awfully stylish gown but she ruins it.

"Robora" doesn't mean red? Well hand me that book again. If those old Carthaginians had as hard a time crossing those mountains as I have digging out this bothersome stuff, I pity them.

Oh, by the way, Mary is going to spent the summer in Switzerland. Going with some old aunt who wants some company and has hysterics or something every few seconds if said company is not agreeable. No thanks. Preserve me from Switzerland if a circumstance like that goes with it.

Oh, dearie me! I believe those old stupids spent more time talking than fighting. Don't believe half these yarns anyway. That vinegar spill is utterly foolish and to think that a Grecian historian—oh yes, Livy was Roman, but there is not a great deal of difference.

Well, it seems to me these words nearly all mean the same thing, "force," "strength" and how you can get a smooth translation for that, I don't see. This is the worry of my life except that dreadful math. and that rhetoric and—. Well it just takes nearly all of my time. When I'm out or any one calls all I can talk about is school and lessons and I'm going to quit studying so hard for I'm not going to be a bore just for lessons. Oh, yes! They undoubtedly do broaden one's mind and perhaps they are worth something.

Did you know Tom Lang was home from school? Nobody knows why. Was out in his new machine the other day and it is too magnificent for words. He can drive it to perfection, too. —"Whose force and strength."

My! I do wish something would happen. School is too dead. Let's get up some elegant new stunt. Really, I think we spend far too much time on our lessons and we don't have enough time for recreation. Wouldn't it be perfectly thrilling if we could do something dreadfully startling. We could—.

What! You don't mean it is that late? Well, I think it is awfully nice studying together, don't you? And it's such a help. I never could have found half those words myself. We must try it again.

M. F. C., '11.

A COLD DAY.

The day is cold and dark and dreary;
It snows and the wind is never weary,
The cars don't stop at the foot of the hill,
So of course we walk, and we walk with a will
But the day is cold and snowy.

My feet are cold and numb and aching;
It snows and the wind long sweeps is making;
My hands are buried deep in my muff;
It seems the cars are all a bluff;
And the day is cold and snowy.

Be still, sad heart! It's not worth minding;
Some where on the track the wheels are grinding;
This fate is the commonest fate of all.
Then do not lament a thing so small,
Though the day be cold and snowy.

Martha Young, '13.

THE YOUNGEST MEMBER OF THE FAMILY.

Tom had been away four years. When at last he came home for a vacation, he could not realize that Margaret, his little sister, whom he had left with braids down her back, had grown any older. One evening, shortly after his arrival, he noticed that Margaret had gone upstairs instead of coming into the parlor after dinner, and said, "Why, where's the kid?"

"O she is going out tonight," said his father.

"Going out!" said Tom, but before his father could answer, the door bell rang and Tom started for the door, think ing, "O well, going to play with some of the youngsters in the neighborhood." As he opened the door he saw John Robbins, an old friend of his.

"Well, hello Old Man, I'm mighty glad to see you, awfully good of you to come and see me so soon. Come up to my room where we can talk over old times.'

"I—", began John.

"O never mind, you can deliver that package any time," said Tom, pointing to a small box under John's arm.

On the stairs they met Margaret who blushed and was about to stop.

"Good bye kid, hope you have a good time," called Tom as he hurried John to his room, and to John, "That's my kid sister, perhaps you don't remember her. Quite a kid when I went away."

John seemed rather ill at ease. "O well," thought Tom, "after he has been here awhile he'll find I haven't changed so much," and he brought his collection of pipes to show John. Presently, however, Tom's father came in and, after greeting John, smilingly remarked, "I knew that Tom would probably keep you all night, so I thought I had better come and get you, as Margaret is afraid you will miss the first act."

"Mar—what? O—er—Are you going—? Well of course I mustn't keep you from—from the first act," finished Tom lamely.

When they had gone, Tom sought his mother with the question, "How old is Margaret, anyway?"

"She is eighteen, only five years younger than you. Not such a baby after all, is she?" replied his mother with a twinkle in her eye.

Tom turned away, muttering "I might have known it was a box of candy under his arm."

Lucy Leyman, '13.

LOVINGLY DEDICATED TO SOUTH HALL GIRLS.

Mice, mice, mice,
Forever and ever it's mice,
Young mice and old mice
And bad mice and bold mice
With sharp teeth and good appetites.
Mice, mice, mice,
Beginning and ending with mice,
You cause consternation,
You rogues of creation,
You mice, mice, mice!

C. L. S., '12.

(With all due apologies to Shakspere.)

To rise or not to rise—that is the question:
Whether 'tis nobler in the mind to go to sleep
With a mouse gnawing in the clothespress by your head,
Or to courageously rise, get your umbrella,
And by heroic battling kill him?
To rise—to kill,—
No more; and by killing to say we end
The gnawing and the thousand startling shocks
The mouse gives rise to—'tis a consummation
Devoutly to be wished! To rise?—or sleep?—
To sleep! perchance to rest! Ay, there's the rub;
For in that rest from toil,
When we have shuffled off our daily care
That mouse may come! There's the respect
That makes calamity of a long night
For who can bear the squeak and squeal of mouse,
Her room-mate's screams and calls to rescue her,
The gnawing of wood, and the mouse
Trying to forage in the waste-basket,
When she herself would take a quiet sleep,
And calm her weary mind? Who would leave her
To chase and kill a harmless mouse
But that the dread of being called a "Coward,"
A hated name that no girl
Wants to bear, spurs her on
And makes her rather rise to kill the mouse
Than sleep, and let him gnaw in peace?
Thus fear of scorn makes martyrs of us all!

C. S., '12.

THE SOROSIS
Published Monthly by the Students of
Pennsylvania College for Women.

Subscriptions to the Sorosis 75 cents per year. Single copies 10c.
Address all business communications to the Business Manager.
Entered in the Postoffice at Pittsburg, Pa., as second-class matter

EDITORIAL.

"Enough of Science and of Art
Close up those barren leaves
Come forth, and bring with you a heart
That watches and receives."

So writes our friend, Mr. Wordsworth of the call of Spring. Translated into practical P. C. W. prose it means, "Spring has come loose your Logics and your Rhetorics and your Mathematics, and cut- cut- cut." At this season of the year, when the hard, long, dreary winter has just been passed, when small boys with kites, tops and marbles, and small maidens with skipping ropes and roller skates, herald the approach of spring we are all alike seized with the same impulse to skip classes and rejoice with nature likewise. Now it is that we are haunted by the long discussed "cut question."

By cuts we mean those dispensations from the faculty which permit a student to absent herself from a stated number of recitations during a semester. Of course all absences are caused only by cases of dire necessity such as severe illness, examinations, etc. Yet, strange as it may seem, there are times when we all prefer "the love which nature brings or a matineé to the most logical lecture in science, even though that matineé may not be so instructive as "The Servant in the House" and "Hedda Gabbler." At such a time how we long for a system of cuts.

This question of cuts has been much discussed by both faculty and students for the adoption of such a rule would be of mutual benefit. In many colleges of high standing the cut system has been tried, successfully; here is has been tried and failed.

The cause of its failure is obvious. At that time the student body of P. C. W. was smaller than it is today and so many classes were necessarily smaller. There are absence of a few students from one class-room often not only inconvenienced the instructor but also hindered the recitation. As a result the cut system was abolished but let us hope not forever.

Within the last few years our number of students has greatly increased, and even greater growth is promised for the future. So the time must surely come when the college will be large enough to turn former failure into success. Then let us be content in looking forward to that happy time when we can adopt that much talked of "cut system."

ALUMNAE.

A number of the Alumnae and Faculty were very pleasantly entertained by Mrs. Walter Dann at her home in Wilkinsburg, on the afternoon of February twelfth.

Born: To Mr. and Mrs. John Houston of Murray Hill avenue on February twenty-third, a son.

Miss Grace Tatnal, who has been teaching in Cincinnati since September, has accepted a position in the High Schools of Harrisburg, where her family has been residing for the past year. Miss Tatnal renewed acquaintances in Pittsburgh and at the College on her way to Harrisburg in the second week of January.

Mr. and Mrs. J. S. Lacock of Farragut street have announced the birth of a son, February eighteenth.

February twenty-sixth a son was born to Mr. and Mrs. Herbert W. Ferry of Poland, Ohio.

Miss Edna McKee attended the dance given by the Freshmen Class, February eighteenth.

COLLEGE NEWS.

The Annual Mid-Year Reception was given by the Faculty of P. C. W. and D. H., Friday evening, February fourth. Berry and South Halls were decorated for the occasion, and were conveniently connected by a canopy. Miss Coolidge and Dr. Lindsay received in the drawing rooms of Berry Hall. The chief feature of the evening was the dancing in Assembly and South Halls. Refreshments were served in the dining room during the evening. The reception was a great success in every respect.

Faculty and students made merry at the Valentine dinner, Friday night, February eleventh. The tables were attractively decorated, as were also the walls, with Valentine day accessories. Heart-shaped dinner cards and a tiny candle and candlestick were at each place. Names had been drawn previously by all, and at the close of the dinner, the presents were distributed. One of the chief enjoyments of the Valentine dinner is the sending back and forth among students and also faculty, of the small heart-shaped candies, containing very tender (?) sentiments.

After dinner, all adjourned to the drawing rooms, where "An Old Sweetheart of Mine" was pleasingly presented in tableaux, Miss Kerst being the reader to the accompaniment of music.

Mrs. Florence Howe Hall lectured to the College and Dilworth Hall, Wednesday morning, February sixteenth. The subject of her lecture was "Famous People I Have Met in My Father's House." Mrs. Hall was brought to the College by the Alumnae Association.

Miss Luella P. Meloy, the instructor of the Social Service classes, lectured to the College, Wednesday morning, February second, on "The Homeless Child." The talk was most interesting and instructive, and convincing.

The Day of Prayer for Colleges was observed Thursday, February tenth, at eleven o'clock. Rev. Alison of the Point Breeze Church, delivered a splendid sermon on "Prayer." Mr. Hamilton of the choir of the Third Presbyterian Church rendered two pleasing solos. After the services, classes were discontinued for the day.

The Sophomore Class repeated the Japanese Operetta "Princess Crysanthemum" on February twenty-sixth, under the auspices of the Alumnae for the benefit of the Dormitory Furnishing Fund.

A Japanese dinner party was given at Miss Coolidge's table, Wednesday evening, February sixteenth, in honor of Miss Coolidge and her guest, Mrs. Florence Howe Hall. Japanese costumes were worn, and the decorations and menu carried out the general Japanese idea.

A Martha Washington party was given in honor of Misses Brownlee and Brownson by the members of their table, Thursday evening, February seventeenth. Colonial gowns were worn, and the table decorations represented camp life at Valley Forge.

A party of College and Dilworth Hall girls visited the Heinz factory, Saturday morning, February nineteenth. They were quite royally entertained and were highly delighted with their trip.

A pleasant little informal tea was given by Miss Elma McKibben, Thursday afternoon, in the dining room of South Hall. The hours were four to six. South Hall girls were the guests.

Mr. Geo. W. Putnam lectured to the College and Faculty, Wednesday morning, February twenty-third. His subject, "Glints of Hope in Drama," is one of peculiar importance to students and theater-goers of the day.

The Freshmen Class entertained the College Friday evening, February eighteenth, in Assembly Hall, at an informal dance. Music was provided by the Junior Band of Braddock, and dainty refreshments were served. The proverbial "green" belonging to Freshmen was the prevailing color.

PERSONALS.

A Sisterly Rebuke.

We are all four happy sisters,
  At the college on the hill.
Pennsylvania is our mother,
  And we love her with a will.

Though we love our youngest sister
  And we're glad that she's so nice,
We would ask her please to listen
  To some sisterly advice.

Please don't think you own our mother's
  Dear old campus, nor her halls,
But remember, there are others
  Who still dwell within her walls.

On your way to recitation
  Try to be not heard, but seen,
And remember, of your sisters
  You're the youngest, dear Thirteen.

A-Nony-Mouse.

Miss Carpenter entertained the Junior Class at a "progressive" luncheon at her home in Wilkinsburg on Saturday, February twenty-sixth. Yellow and white tulips were the favors.

Miss Clarissa Blakeslee has taken up her school duties again after an illness of several weeks.

Miss Hamilton, translating French in History class—"Richelieu's aim was to put down the House of Ostrich."

In a history recitation—"The people of Milan had to give in after they starved to death."

To Mr. Putnam in English class—"Isn't it easy to win love?"

Miss Diescher can't quite see the difference between a warship and a worship!

On Valentine's Day the Juniors entertained at luncheon in honor of the birthdays of Miss McClymonds and Miss Carpenter. Miss Brownson, who is their honorary member, was also present. The decorations were hearts and arrows.

In history—"Henry's death was the one great obstacle in his way."

Miss Florence Bickel entertained the Sophomores at a Valentine Party on Saturday afternoon, February twelfth, in her room in South Hall.

At a tea given by Mrs. Vernon Charnley at her home in Rosslyn Farms on February fifth, the engagement of her sister, Miss Marion Knapp of Sewickley to Mr. Walter MacGregor of Chicago was announced.

The Sorosis wishes to join in the general welcome extended to Miss Charlotte W. Hazelwood of Boston, who comes as a new member of our Faculty. She comes to fill the position of Greek and Latin instructor, left vacant by Miss Green.

Mrs. Armstrong has moved over to South Hall to be "one of us." We all wish to extend her a hearty welcome, and we feel that Berry Hall's loss is South Hall's gain.

On Thursday, March third, an unusually large audience was gathered in the library to hear Mr. Henry George, Jr. Owing to the splendid street-car service of this city the lecturer was somewhat belated but his audience were well repaid for their patience. Mr. Henry George is the son of the late Mr. Henry George of New York City, who led the single-tax movement. Mr. George, Jr., is also a firm upholder of this principle. He lectured on Japan, where he has been a newspaper correspondent for several years. Being a close observer, Mr. George gave us vivid pictures of all phases of life there, political, educational, and social. He discussed the wonderful progress Japan has made and showed how she too is confronted today with the same questions which the United States must face.

Mrs. Eddy, a missionary doing work in India, spoke to the house girls on "India", Sunday, February sixth, at Vesper Service.

Dr. Lindsay addressed the Y. W. C. A. Tuesday evening, February first.

The house girls have been deriving a great deal of pleasure from skating on the tennis courts during the cold weather. When flooded, the courts are capable of rivaling Duquesne Garden.

Mrs. McHenry of Washington, Pa., visited her daughter, Lillian, in South Hall, Saturday and Sunday, February twelfth and thirteenth.

Dr. J. C. Stahlmann of Vandergrift, Pa., visited his daughter, Calla, Wednesday evening, February ninth.

Miss Elsie Weihe entertained her mother and sister of Connellsville, Pa., Saturday and Sunday, February twelfth and thirteenth, in South Hall.

Misses Ruby McCullough and Agnes Murray of Kittanning, Pa., were guests of Miss Titzell and Miss Young, for the Valentine dinner and the week-end.

Miss Jean McCague of Sewickley was the guest of her sister, Elizabeth, at the Valentine dinner.

Miss Brownson spent the week-end, February eleventh-fourteenth, at her home in Washington, Pa., attending the Brownson reunion.

Miss Marguerite Titzell entertained Misses Ionia Smith, Louise Fletcher and Esther O'Neill at her home in Kittanning, during the mid-year vacation, January twenty-eighth-thirty-first.

Miss Jane Hill of Carnegie and Miss Jean Hughes of Latrobe were guests at the Valentine dinner, Friday, February eleventh.

Miss Merna Stahlmann, a student at Indiana Normal, spent Sunday, February twenty-seventh, in South Hall, with her sister, Calla.

Misses Evelyn Crandall, Calla Stahlmann, and Hazel Hall spent a week-end during the middle of February at the home of Miss Marie Shinn at Carnegie. Miss Shinn was a student of Dilworth Hall last year.

Our readers will be sorry to learn that as we go to press, our editor, Miss Tassey, is in great sorrow in the death of her father, Mr. Hugh Tassey, who passed away on Wednesday, March ninth. Miss Tassey has the sincere sympathy of all her college friends.

MUSIC NOTES.

The Mandolin Club played on the Washington's Birthday program at the United Presbyterian Home for the Aged in Wilkinsburg. The exercises were in charge of the Auxiliary Board of the Home of which Miss McQuiston is a member.

The College Glee Club gave its second annual concert at Kingsley House, February sixteenth. The large audience was enthusiastic and seemed to especially enjoy the College Songs. Light refreshments and an informal dance followed the concert.

EXCHANGES.

The January Exchanges were for the most part bright and attractive. Many contained pleasing short stories and commendable serious literary material. It is to be deplored that a number of papers lack an Exchange Department. It is this section of the paper that especially interests other Exchange Editors and it should by no means be omitted. All Editors are anxious to know whether their efforts are successful or not, and it is in the Exchange columns that they look for praise or condemnation.

The Washington-Jeffersonian always comes forward with a lot of things that are "worth while."

We gladly welcome the reappearance of the Journal of Blairsville College, which has been discontinued for a year. All success to you.

College publications seem to be unanimous in desiring to boom the Short Story Department. The enterprise is laudable and should be encouraged but we must not forget to insist upon maintaining a high standard.

There was a young fellow named Wright
Who studied the birds in their flight.
"If these sparrows can fly,
Why in thunder can't I?"
Quoth he and he proved he was right.

At the Box Office.

Lady (timidly)—I'd like two seats for four weeks from tonight.

Ticket Seller (sternly)—See here, madam, in New York you can't go to the theater on the spur of the moment like that.

A lady on board suddenly approached the Captain:

"Please tell me, sir," she asked timidly, "what time the boat starts."

"It starts, madam, when I give the word," was the haughty reply.

"Oh, indeed! I thought it started when the engineer pulled the lever. Thank you very much."

POTTERY
Hamilton & Clark Co.
208 OLIVER AVENUE
NEW LOCATION
CHINA
GLASS

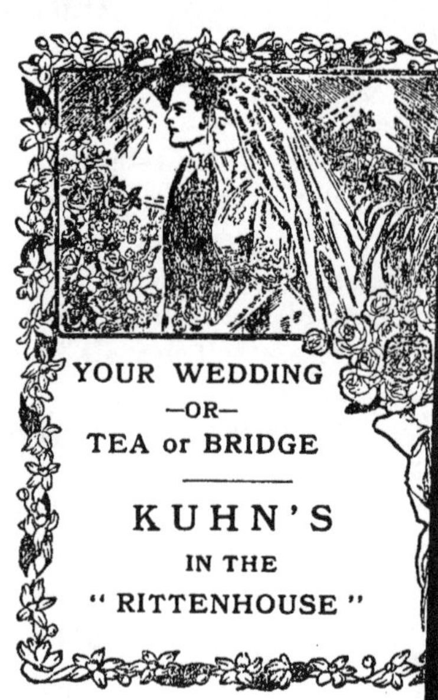
YOUR WEDDING
—OR—
TEA or BRIDGE
KUHN'S
IN THE
"RITTENHOUSE"

THE SOROSIS

VOL. XVI MARCH, 1910 No. 5

THE PSYCHOLOGY OF PUBLIC SPEAKING.

People in general are afraid of the term psychology, and this common prejudice is well founded and easily understood. The science was founded by Aristotle, who defined it as the science of the soul in a treatise too abstract and difficult for the comprehension of an ordinary man. Later all sorts of thinks such as telepathy, hypnotism, double personality were presented under the names of psychology. But now it is one of the most praetical and fascinating of all the sciences as taught to-day. Psychology is a systematic study of the human mind, and it is the public speaker's whole task to influence this mind.

Ordinarily we have no means for knowing the forms in which our companions do their thinking. We know the results of their mental processes, and it is only the results that we are usually interested in. We hardly know our own methods and take it for granted that all think alike. But each one sees different things; to one the world is a panorama; to another, a series of sounds; to another it is primarily an organism of movements. Every public speaker is naturally inclined to appeal to that form of imagery which impresses him most but that form may be meanginless to his hearers. But great orators make frequent use of diversified forms of mental imagery though visual imagery is used as much as all the others combined. It is by means of the imagination that we grasp reality for ourselves, and it is by this means that we reveal it to others. The imagination is not for the purpose of deception, but for the more worthy end of revelation. The imagination has a high place in the emotions. The public speaker tries to awaken the emotions, but he can only do this by presenting concrete situation to the mind. The emotions are stirred by objects present to the senses or by such objects as can easily be imagined. That which I do not perceive or that of which I have no distinct mental image, is incapable of awakening my emotions. The public speaker must learn never to attempt to arouse the emotions of his hearers without presenting the emotional object so clearly that they are capable of forming a vivid mental image of it. We enjoy descriptions which awaken our prevailing form of imagery, but those that demand for their interpretation forms of imagery which we do not possess displease us. We become wearied with the use of one sense organ and seek rest by the use of the other senses, so a continuous appeal to our prevailing form of imagery would become monotonous and would not reveal the whole truth. Innitilian defined the orator as a good man prepared to speak and no man is completely equipped to speak to reveal the full truth with all its convincing power, who is not able to clothe it in all the available forms of mental imagery. New forms of mental imagery may be developed, but unless they are developed early in life they never reach a high degree of proficiency.

We understand the emotions by experiencing them. But voluntary production of the symptoms of an emotion tends to make the emotion a reality. So we have the attitude of worship insisted upon by our churches. Shakespeare expressed a great truth when he said, "Assume a virtue if you have it not." The assumption tends to make the virtue a reality. There are diverse opinions among great actors as to whether the emotions as they portray them are real or assumed. But there is much evidence to support the theory that the way to move an audience is first to move yourself. The methods of expressing and interpreting the expressions of emotions is a subject of interest to all and has been discussed for many centuries. But it seems now that nothing helpful on the subject could have been produced until there was recognition of the evolutions of man, and of the close relationship between the mind and the body. To understand the expressions we must know how the emotions were evolved and hence what physical symptoms each emotion must have. Spencer says: "The violence of the physical expressions is in proportion to the intensity of the emotion. Expressions of emotions must not be overdone. Many actors are criticised as tearing a passion to tatters because their bodily actions are in excess of what should ordinarily accompany any particular degree of emotion. We object to exaggeration in certain emotions very much more than others. Joy may be overdone with impunity where an equal exaggeration of sorrow would produce disgust. In the beginning of an address or play the audience is not fully in sympathy with the speaker, so it is dangerous to attempt any extreme emotion involving pain or sorrow. It is better to fail to make the audience laugh with you than to fail to make it weep with you. Ordinarily the first emotion appealed to should be one of pleasantness. If this is successful there is formed a sympathy between the speaker and his audience which makes appeals to the sadder emotions much less hazardous.

It has been proved that the functions of the mind like the heart and lungs are unable to continue their activity for more than short periods of time. Every period of activity is followed by a period of rest. All our thinking is done in "spurts" which are uniformly followed by periods of inactivity. In public addresses it is seldom that we are able to hold the full and undivided attention for more than a few seconds or minutes at best. No one can attend to what we are saying or doing unless we are presenting a new aspect of the subject every few seconds. The unit of our thinking is not the letter or the word, but the simple sentence or clause. Often we do not know what is being said until the end of the sentence or clause and then our minds run back and get the import of the whole. In general each single sentence requires a "spurt" of attention and the presentation must conform to this psycholological fact. Every lecturer or entertainer must also expect a gradual rise and fall of the intensity and duration of those recurrent "spurts" of attention, and so must adjust his lecture to the actual mental limitations of his hearers.

All motions are vibratory, and yet the fact often escapes us entirely. There are regularly recurring periods in the solar system and these have untold influence upon the life of all plants and animals. Rhythm is not confined at all to the celestial bodies, but is found everywhere, and as man's development depends on his adjustment to his environment, it is expected that all minds will be peculiarly susceptible to the influence of that which pervades and rules in the heavens, and the earth, in the mind and the body. Primitive peoples used rhythm in their actions and performances; children, peasants, sale criers, hawkers, and evangelists all use and are influenced by rhythm. We may not be aware that we are influenced by rhythm, but we may be so under the influence of the rhythm of the voice that our bodies sway in sympathetic movements and our emotions are excited to the utmost. Appeals must be made by the speaker to the attention and rhythm when properly regulated makes just the right frequency of appeals, hence the results are highly satisfactory.

To discuss the subject of suggestion some attention must be given to hypnotism because it is here alone that uggestion is fully manifested. But suggestion can be made without hypnotism usually on peculiarly suggestible subjects. There are two characteristics to suggestion: The thought or action must be suggested by some external stimulus. Then the idea suggested results in action or belief without the ordinary amount of deliberation or criticism. Man has been considered a logical machine, but the more modern conception of man is that he is a creature who rarely reasons at all. Our most important actions are performed and our most sacred conceptions are reached by means of the merest suggestion. In moving and inspiring men suggestion is to be considered as in every way the equal of logical ages, but the emotions play a striking part in awakening the images. Logical processes of thought are practically devoid of reasoning. Public speakers must limit the consciousness of the minds of the hearers to the idea suggested and avoid ideas in their minds which invalidate or hinder the ideas suggested.

To render an audience suggestible a speaker must avoid their suspicion or secure their confidence. He must be regarded by his audience as an authority and this is more easily gained by formality. He must be formally introduced. Repetition is a good method for suggestibility. As Mr. Dooley says: "I belave annything at all, if ye only tell it to me often enough." Figures of speech are always effective, especially the metaphor of which Mr. Bryan is master. Of the greatest importance is indirect suggestion or suggesting the conclusion so the hearer can reach the desired conclusion before it is expressed by the speaker, and when the point is asserted the hearer receives it as a confirmation of the conclusion which he had already formed in his own mind.

The thousands of people we see on the streets every day form a heterogeneous crowd because the purpose which animates each is unknown to the others, and the action of each is largely independent of the others. But this crowd may be turned into a homogeneous crowd by an event which would occupy the attention of all and unify their purpose. A homogeneous crowd demands a leader. The crowd is like primitive man in its thinking and acting. Reason does not enter in to restrain action, to criticise suggested ideas or to hinder self-surrender to absorbing emotions. The crowd thinks in images and is incapable of abstract logical thought. Images succeed one another in the most illogical order and lead to fantastical situations and conclusions, but the fallacy of the process of thinking is never evident to the crowd. The crowd is a group of individuals in a heightened state of suggestibility.

Every audience is either a heterogeneous or homogeneous crowd. It is never completely heterogeneous and the highest degree of homogeneity of a crowd is secured only under the influence of a speaker, and so when it is an audience. The most difficult task is not to convince and sway the crowd, but to create it. Since a community of experience and purpose is needed the orator may assume a certain degree of uniformity of experience, but he must state their problems, aspiration and puroses in such a way that each will feel that that which is said appeals to all in the same way and that it is but the expression of the purpose and ideas of each. One of the best methods of changing an audience into a crowd is to have them sit close together. The touching of elbows adds to the consciousness of the presence of others in a way that cannot be secured in any other manner. One student of crowds states that it would be impossible to have a crowd of angels because they could not feel the bodily presence of others. Another method is ritual. Have all rise, sit, read, sing together. A good way is to have the crowd cheer early in the performance. Either have them applaud the speaker as he steps out or tell a funny story. The unity of the crowd consists more in identity of feeling than if ideas, hence applause is more effective than ritual.

The great orator knows instinctively how to deal with the crowd. He must make his appeal to the mind of the crowd as it is and not as we might assume it to be, from knowing the individuals composing it. The crowd, like primitive man, thinks in images rather than in logical processes. The skillful orator awakens these images one after another, or holds a single picture so vividly before the crowd that the results, image or images, become as realities and lead to the most extreme measures to carry out that which is merely imagined. A leader of a crowd must have a vivid imagination and must be able to awaken such images in the minds of his hearers. When an orator has welded his audience into a homogeneous crowd he must never be guilty of reasoning with them, for he has taken away their faculty of reasoning by making a crowd. He should affirm reasonable things and affirm conclusions which he has come to by processes of reasoning. Not only do crowds think in images but the emotions play a striking part in awakening images. Logical processes of thought are practically devoid of emotional coloring, which the conclusions reached by primitive man and by crowds are the results of feeling rather than of reasoning. Orators must stir the emotions, hence successful leaders of crowds are highly emotional by nature and surpass others in moving the feelings of their hearers.

Elma McKibben, '10.

---

*THE SOUL OF A VIOLIN.

By Frances Alden Cameron, '11.

Hand in hand before the dying glow of the fire light, sat the Musician and his wife, their wistful old faces exquisitely defined against the dark background of their chairs, their eyes half closed and tender with the spell of dreams. Upon the musician's lap, lay a beautiful old violin, quaintly carved and

*Honorable mention in Short Story Contest.

perfectly formed in the manner of long ago, perhaps by the hand of the Master, himself, for the magical name of Cremona lay engraved with the date inside; the musician's fingers caressed the instrument in a manner which was at once both tender and reverent, yet there was infinite sadness in the touch, and the little melody which he had just finished playing had been filled with sadness too, though he had meant it to be otherwise.

The room where the two sat was a small one and barely furnished. The snow lay sifted in tiny piles about the window sill, and the wind swept about the corners of their attic walls, and seemed almost to force an entrance through the poorly fitting panes of glass. Upon the wall, over the mantel piece, hung a large portrait and through the soft haze of firelight, a girl's bright face smiled down from its gilded frame and seemed almost a living presence within the room. The two old people by the fire sat often with their tear dimmed eyes, gazing up into the brown ones over head, drinking in all the beautiful lines and curves of the portrait, and speaking of it, as though she were a living thing. For so she had dwelt and smiled down upon them for almost nineteen years, always the same little maid who had gone out from their presence, nineteen summers before. It was the altar of the musician's home, the beautiful old mansion which had dwindled down to two small attic rooms, and it was always in front of her little girl's portrait that the mother had dreamt her tenderest dreams, and lived her happiest moments, living and yearning for the accomplishment of her life's one prayer—and here also was where the musician had composed his most beautiful melodies—those which were filled with the hidden pathos that but few can understand. For here she must find them waiting when she came back again, their arms and faces—full of welcome, and the same old love which had never once failed her during the years of separation, to be her portion once more. For come back to them she must, and they would always be ready to receive her as though she had only slipped away for a little while, and would come back again as she had gone away—the same old light in her eyes. Every evening, just at twilight, the musician and his wife would sit together before the fire and he would play and she would sing, in her low little crooning way the quaint old airs, their child had loved—in the dear old long ago. It was the happiest hour in the whole day to both, for the firelight is full of love and dreams—and out of the fading coals came soft melodies and tender thoughts which were dear to both, and sweeter still, through the soft mists of the twilight, the spirit of their lost child seemed often to come back and slip her hands in theirs. They could almost hear her whisper—"Father and mother, dear—it is I, your little girl who has come back to you." And the girl in the golden frame—smiled down upon them, with her same old merry look, as though she had heard it all—and really understood.

* * * * * * * * * * * * *

But the twilights of late had seemed each one—to have grown more lonely than the one before, though now they were filled with the presence of sadness—and often while she listened, the wifes eyes would fill with tears—and more than once the melody which the musician played—would end in a strain of such deep and terrible longing that the musician would at last be forced to throw his instrument aside—lest it become an unconscious betrayer of the great sorrow within his heart.

"For her sake," he would whisper—"Oh, God, in Heaven, for her sake bring back the child who has gone away." So every night, while she sank to sleep—lulled by the voice of her beloved Cremona, the old musician would blend each song into a prayer, not that the fading life, of her whom he knew and loved so well, be spared and given back to him again. He was too noble even in the midst of his grief to wish that she be given back to the life of privation and suffering which she had endured, during the past years. He merely prayed that if such a thing were possible now, the girl who had left them one early morning, nineteen summers before, might be given back for a little while. When at last, he too, clearly saw and realized that which he had feared and dreaded so long, he uttered no cry, he fought no battle such as other men have fought and won in the presence of that stranger who robs us of those we love best. He simply knelt and pressed his lips quite reverently against his wife's hand, and she woman-like, realizing all that which he could not speak, said softly:

"Do not worry, my sweetheart, for she is coming back again. Perhaps, while I am here. Perhaps when I am gone, to comfort you;—and I am happy now—and so must you be also."

* * * * * * * * * * * * *

The days and weeks slipped quickly by, and she steadily grew worse. There was no outward pain—only the deep longing in her dark eyes whenever she looked up at her child's portrait and met the girlish eyes. But presently this too passed away and her greatest pleasure was to lie and listen to the violin, whose music she craved both day and night—that, and the light of her husband's face.

There came a day—when there was no longer any food in the house—no coal for the tiny grate, and no money with which to buy the medicine upon which alone she lived. They were strangers in the city, the theater where he had played of late was now closed for at least a month's repairs—and he had absolutely no way in which to procure or borrow enough money with which to prolong his wife's life. He left her for a little while to fight out his battle alone. There were two things, either of which he might sell and procure the medicine and simple luxuries which were necessary—the portrait of his daughter Cicely, and that which had always seemed dearer to him than life itself, the violin of Cremona.

The portrait was framed in a gold frame of exceptional value. Above all it had been designed and painted by a great artist whose name should have brought it a goodly sum had the portrait no other value. If he sent her portrait away, it would be almost as though he were sending the child herself away, and destroying the last beautiful memory which bound them to the past. His wife's last words came back to him: "I am never lonely when Cicely is here," and it felt that it had been decided for him and her portrait could not be sold. But the violin!

When he came back to the attic rooms he had a smile all ready to greet his wife and a smile for the child in the golden frame.

"I am going out on a little errand, sweetheart," said he bravely, yet with averted eyes—"I will not be gone long."

"Yes," she answered dreamily—her voice coming from far away. "But play one little song for me before you go. I am so tired, dear lover, I think it would play me to sleep."

It was one of their favorite songs which the musician chose to play for her that night—Rubenstein's Meldy in F, that song of dreams and wistful fancies which we all love and never can too often hear, and the musician played it as though he stood in another world and the angels were guiding his fingers. Afterwards he drifted into Mendelssohn's beautiful old Spring Song, and while he played, the tired look left his wife's face and she smiled in her sleep as though she were back in the past again. The musician closed the door very softly behind him, his cheek still resting upon the beloved Cremona as though upon the face of the child one touches for the last time—and so passed out into the night. He took the violin to a former patron of his—who wondered at the deep sorrow written upon the old man's tired face, asked no question, but wrote out a check for five hundred dollars. The violin was worth more than that, it had been an heirloom in the musician's family for many generations. The musician reached the door, but turned and blindly stretching out a hand of thanks to his friend, Thurston, he fought back the tears which involuntarily rose to his eyes and said—in his quiet way—"The bow of ribbon—please leave it there, on the violin. My little girl tied it on the summer before she was taken away, and we have always left it there for Cicely's sake. Just a fancy, you know, but I could never bear to think of our—the violin without it—and the touch of her little hands."

"It shall always remain there," answered the other kindly. "And you must always feel free to come back and play whenever you care to upon your old violin. Some time, I dare say, you will have it your own again."

When the musician reached his home a short time afterward, his wife still slept, but woke to greet him with her usual bright smile.

"Dear," she called softly from the other room, "I am much better now, I have had such a beautiful long rest and all I want is for you to play to me—some little song, which our Cicely loved."

The musician came over to his wife's side and laid his hands tenderly upon her forehead. Through the soft twilight haze, their eyes met. "Sweetheart," he said bravely, smiling wistfully down into her brown eyes, "I cannot play for you tonight."

She died a few nights afterward. There was no pain, but a gradual sinking into slumber—her hand resting unto the very last against her husband's face. Just at the close she roused herself from the lethergy into which she had fallen and said: "Some time, when you need me most, I will come back to you from the spirit world. I know not how—but call me when you need me and I shall come. I should know your voice through all eternity—your voice and the sound of your violin."

(To be continued.)

A FAVOR RETURNED.

Once upon a time there stood among the blue hills of Kentucky a little red brick inn, nestling cosily under its low roof of thatch. The tiny black and scarlet sign swinging over the door informed one that this hostelry was called "Traveler's Rest" and that its keeper was Sophy Johnson.

Old Sophy, however, had relinquished most of the care of the inn, which was not great, to her one and only daughter, Maud, for she had attained to that ripe old age when a soft seat in the chimney corner was desirable above all else. She most enjoyed the time well on in the evening when the work was all done, and the room was pleasantly warmed and lighted by the dying embers.

She was sitting thus one cold blustering evening, her daughter at her side, discussing the cruel war that was devastating the country and impoverishing the people. The long quivering shadows flickered on the great chests in the four corners of the room and crept in and out among the strings of dried fish that hung from the rafters. When Maud was younger many a time in a game of hide and seek, had she and her comrades taken refuge upon those great rafters, in the little dark recess between them and the sloping roof.

"Ah me," sighed the woman lifting her wasted hands and letting them fall into her lap again, " 'tis a hard life at best for a poor widow to lead and now when the soldiers are so near and ready to snatch the very food from one's mouth—" she shook her head and gazed into the glowing embers.

" 'Twas only this morning old Peter told me the Confederates won at Fredericksburg and our soldiers had fled to Washington. Ah," she sighed, "I know it cannot last" and the old dame sank back in her chair, shaking her head mournfully as she thought of peaceful days long past.

"But come!" she said rousing herself at last, "let us lock the door for the night. Surely no one will come to the Inn now. Hear the wind! And the sign over the door, how it creaks!"

The two arose and stood listening. Suddenly Maud cried, "That is not the wind, mother! There is some one without!"

Almost instantly the door burst open and with a rush of snow and sleet a union soldier entered dragging a chest behind him and stood looking doubtfully at the two standing in the red fire-light. Maud spoke first.

" 'Tis but a poor night for travelers, sir," she said, coming forward.

"Yes, yes. But for some there is no choice," answered the man in a solemn tone.

The old dame hobbled forward.

"Sit there by the fire, sir, and Maud shall brew you some tea."

"No, no!" cried the soldier, "I have no time for that! I must find a hiding place quick!"

"A hiding place?" repeated Maud.

"Yes, yes, and be quick! Oh, you must! You do not understand. I must have a hiding place for myself and this box."

"He wants a hiding place, mother," explained Maud.

"What! What! Maud? A hiding place!" murmured the woman excitedly.

"My good woman, oh, do not hesitate," cried the man, "you shall be repaid a thousand times if only you hide me safely this night."

"What shall we do?" cried the old lady in dismay wringing her hands.

At this juncture a loud knock was heard and a voice crying, "Let me in! Let me in!"

"Oh heavens!" gasped the man with an agonized look about him. Quick as a flash he reached high above his head and placed his burden on one of the rafters and drew himself up beside it above the swaying garlands of fish.

The land lady slowly and tremblingly drew the bolt and admitted three other men. One stepped forward and it was plain to see he was worn out.

"I suppose you wish rooms for the night," said Maud as calmly as she could. But it was well for her the firelight was growing dim or her glowing face would have betrayed her.

"Yes, I dare say we will," answered the one lightly, "but you may as well produce that fellow, we know he is here and we are bound to have him."

"Is he asking after the gentleman?" asked old Sophy, hobbling forward. Events had occurred in too rapid succession for her slow brain to untangle.

"Yes, mother that gentleman who stopped here this afternoon," answered Maud hastily. "You'll have to hurry, sir, to catch him," she added, turning to the guests, "for he rode off on the best horse in these parts."

"Pretty well done, my dear, pretty well done. Not well enough though, to fool us. I had him but a stone's throw before me until darkness and this confounded snow fell and then I lost him."

"Then it could not have been he who was here for he was gone full three hours ago," answered Maud.

"So, so?" replied the man, "we'll see what the old woman says. Here, my kind soul," he shouted, "where's that man you are hiding?"

" 'Deed sir, would that I knew!" grumbled the old lady. "I just turned about for a second and when I looked at him again he was gone."

"Nothin' from her either," growled the men. "Now, see here, you two," said one, "I'm done with this foolin'. I'm goin' to search this place."

Sophy rose and led the men out of the room. When they had gone through the other three rooms the same man said gruffly, "I'll let the house stand for tonight, for we want a place to sleep but in the morning—it burns," and he nodded his head significantly.

Early the next morning Maud was dressed and in the living room.

"Sir!" she whispered softly.

"Here I am," and the man swung down quickly and brought his box.

"Come out; you're not safe in the daytime up there. You must ride away from her at once," and Maud led him down the road to the next house where stood in the rear four farm horses.

"They are not swift bu tthey are strong and can carry you all day if need be," she said burying her hand in their thick manes. So saying she sprang lightly on the broad back of one, the man followed her example and both trotted down the road.

After what seemed an age to them, Maud led her horse between two hills, pointed to a jungle of matted grasses and said, "You will be perfectly safe here."

"Why, where, I do not see," and the man gazed where her finger pointed again.

The girl laughed merrily. "That is just the point," she said. "One doesn't see it until he has been here many, many times. But watch." She pushed a stone or two away. An opening appeared large enough to admit the man and the horse.

"You must go in there and stay until you think I have had time to start the other men on their way," she explained.

"How can I ever repay you?" he asked, and then added, "This box here contains bills, money, and if I do not come back from the war it shall be yours. Those men pursuing me were after it. They have no right to it, it was given to me." And with Maud's help he carefully concealed the treasure in the little cave. She gave him some bread and cheese and hurried home to allay the suspicions of his pursuers.

* * * * * * * * * * * * *

Many years passed. The cruel war ended with the union victorious. Old Sophy, the innkeeper, had joined the realm of departed souls. Maud still lived at the old place, which was no longer an inn but her home for her husband and children.

She often thought of the man whom she had aided long ago and she wondered if he were ever coming again to claim his money. He had said if he did not come again it should be hers.

Sitting one evening with her husband in front of the house she suddenly turned, "Will," she said, "you know years ago during the war mother and I helped one of our soldiers to hide and to conceal some money he had."

"Yes?" said Will, interested.

"Well, when he went back to the war he said if he didn't come again the money should be ours, and he has never returned."

"What! Why did you never tell me? Where did you hide it?" asked Will, much excited.

"I always thought he would come," said Maud, "but now I don't know, it has been so long," and she shook her head doubtfully.

"He said it should be mine," she continued, "and we need it so badly."

"Yes," Will replied, "I think it should be ours. He will not come now. We will look for it tomorrow morning."

The next morning, Maud again led the way down the road to the old place between the two hills. She rolled the stones away and she and Will entered the tiny cave. Carefully she uncovered the box and Will lifted it and bore it out of the cave. "Let's open it right here," said Maud, much excited.

Will was speechless. He set the box down and began to undo the cords that bound it. He removed the lid.

"Oh!" cried both at once, as Will held up a handful of bills. They never were more disappointed in their ilves.

"Yes," said Will, "no wonder your soldier never returned. It is Confederate money and not worth a cent."

Beulah Pierce, '12.

COLLEGE TRIALS.

As I sat in meditation,
Hoping for an inspiration
Bright and gay,
Nothing came but lamentation
For eight-thirty recitation
Every day.

Every morning bright and early
Maidens with locks straight and curly,
Climb the hill.
Up the endless steps they hasten,
Climbing toward their destination
Fit to kill.

For the street car each has waited
With her zeal all unabaited
Till it came.
Early rose each from her slumber,
Conquered drawbacks without number,
Fog and rain.

Yet, relentlessly, the teacher
Looks "a hole through" each poor creature
Who is late.
Why should so much tribulation
Enter into education?
It is fate!

F. K. W., '11.

A FABLE.

Once upon a time a Geometry and a Cicero, finding themselves left alone in a room for a few minutes began a conversation. After they had exchanged a few commonplace remarks, the Geometry said, "Oh, my friend, you have a happy time. The same girl owns us both, but how differently she treats us. She likes to study you, therefore she treats you with some consideration, but me—!" Here the poor Geometry choked with emotion, and became silent. "Yes," answered the Cicero, "I have noticed that she treats you rather rudely, but then she is only thoughtless, I am sure that you could be treated much worse.

"I don't see how," indignantly responded the Geometry. "She jerks me open and slams me shut. Several of the vertebrae of my back are sprained, and one of my sides is dislocated.

In the pause that followed, a book from a neighboring desk spoke. "Pardon me," it said, "but I could not help overhearing you.—I am a Biology. My owner hates me and sometimes never touches me for weeks, so that my back becomes stiff from want of exercise, and then almost breaks when at last I am opened. Besides this, I am very sensitive, and my owner's attitude toward me hurts me cruelly. You," it continued, turning to the Geometry, "should be very happy, for it is only your back that is injured, while not only my back, but alas, my heart also is broken."

Maude Shutt, '13.

THE MUSIC OF THE RAIN.

The rain is dripping, dropping down;
The sky is leaden gray,
And swollen streamlets everywhere
Rush madly on their way.

The trees stretch forth their tender buds
To drink the sparkling drops.
A vapor cloaks in silver mist
The trembling lilac tops.

A soft veil hovers o'er the hills
And o'er the silent turn,
Seen dimly through the fading light,
As twilight filters down.

A melody floats in the air,
Low, with a soft refrain;
Soon weary ones are lulled to rest
By the music of the rain. '11.

THE SOROSIS
Published Monthly by the Students of
Pennsylvania College for Women.
Ethel Tassey, 10 .... Editor-in-Chief
Elma McKibben, 10 .... Business Manager
Minerva Hamilton, '11 .... Literary Editor
Elvira Estep, '12 .... College Notes
Calla Stahlman, '12 .... Personals
Lillian McHenry, '13 .... Exchanges
Gertrude Wayne, '11 .... Assistant Business Manager
Subscriptions to the Sorosis 75 cents per year. Single copies 10c.
Address all business communications to the Business Manager.
Entered in the Postoffice at Pittsburg, Pa., as second-class matter

PATRIOTISM.

"St. Patrick's Day in the Morning!"

On the seventeenth day of March every Irishman proudly displays his shamrock or bit of green of some kind. No matter in what part of the world he may be, his patriotic heart is with "Dear Old Ireland;" not one particular section, but the whole of the Emerald Isle.

Loyalty to the entire nation as a nation, without regard to particular people, parties or divisions of country constitutes ideal patriotism. For more than half a century the United

States has been unquestionably a perfect union and in international relations American patriotism is all that can be desired; it is at home that the weakness crops out. All talk of a division between the North and the South has long ago ceased but we still hear of the "Solid South" and still find politicians anxiously watching how the new president will be received in general on his southern tour.

The most definite expression of any such feeling centers about the song "Dixie." It is a stirring tune, liked by everybody but certainly does not merit the rank of a national anthem, or a substitute for one. At the last presidential inauguration it was a common thing for a band to interrupt whatever it happened to be playing and dash into "Dixie". The crowd would shout like mad. The instant the music changed to "Yankee Doodle" or "America" the clamor ceased and the feeble echo that followed was so faint and short-lived as to cause the few broad-minded patriots to give up the useless struggle in disgust. Washington might be a Southern city, but Mr. Taft was being inaugurated President of the United States.

This state of affairs may be the result of our lack of a national anthem of our own. The question of such an anthem has been talked up for years, it seems as if it is time to do something now. We have used "God Save the King" long enough. Our country has taken its place among the first nations of the world in other respects and can't afford to have a reproach of any kind on its patriotism.

ALUMNÆ.

Decade Club II met at the home of Mrs. Verne Shear in Wilkinsburg the Second Friday in March. They continued their study of the essayists, and planned to undertake some sewing for the Homeopathic Hospital during the spring months.

Miss Georgia Negley, who has been very ill, is improving.

Mrs. Charles L. Taylor is spending the spring with her daughter in New Jersey.

Mrs. George Porter, Mrs. W. S. Miller, and Mrs. Charles Spencer were among the alumnae who attended Mr. George's lecture on "Japan."

Mrs. John M. Pardee is improving after her severe illness.

COLLEGE NOTES.

On Wednesday morning, March ninth, Madame de Vallay talked to the college about her life as a French girl and later as an American woman. Time was lacking and she could not finish her talk, but we hope to have an opportunity soon to hear the conclusion. There are few who have had so many interesting experiences in a life time as Madame de Valley.

Omega Society held an open meeting in the Drawing Rooms, on Thursday afternoon, March tenth. The program was highly interesting and very original. Dainty refreshments were served after the program in the Reception Room.

A party of girls from the college and Dilworth Hall had an interesting trip through the Ward-Mackey Company building on Friday evening, March eleventh.

We were all very much interested in Dr. Bryan's talk on "Japan," which he delivered to the college on the sixteenth of March. He has been a missionary in Japan for many years, and so was well acquainted with his subject.

Everybody was delighted with the presentation of "The Cricket on the Hearth," by the graduating class of Dilworth Hall on March eighteenth and nineteenth.

The dining room of Berry Hall presented a vivid atmosphere at dinner on St. Patrick's Day. Each table had a party of its own, and had green decorations in the shape of hats, pipes, shamrocks, and everything else suggesting St. Patrick and the good old Emerald Isle.

Miss Coolidge entertained the Omega Society at dinner Thursday evening, March tenth. Mr. and Mrs. Putnam were also guests. The decorations were prettily carried out in daffodils and in gold and white, the colors of the society. After dinner the guests entertained themselves by writing novels, some of which were highly dramatic.

Thursday afternoon, March seventeenth, the College German Club held its first regular meeting in the Senior Parlor. Gertrude Wayne, '11, president of the society, presided and Miss Skilton, honorary member of the society, was present. A pleasant hour was passed in discussion of German customs, and in playing German games. Truly Deutsch refreshments were served. The society has made some interesting plans for the future.

PERSONALS.

Miss Amelia Horst was the guest of Miss Anna Larimer, at her home in West Newton, Pa., for the week end, March eleventh-fourteenth.

Mrs. C. D. Crandell, of Warren, Pa., visited her daughter, Evelyn, in South Hall for the week of March third-eleventh.

Miss Martha Young spent the week end, March eighteenth-twenty-first, at her home in Vandergrift, Pa.

Miss Ionia Smith spent the week end, March eighteenth-twentieth, with Miss Jean Marshall of Rochester, Pa.

Miss Stahlmann—"Starch is a very good food."

Heard in the "Den"—"What did Chaucer do when he came back from his first missionary journey?" Evidently a Sophomore.

The Sophomores have adopted a new motto:
"Cultivate a sweet smile and a straight back-bone."
Heard in Labratory—
Miss Hogue—Did I cut out your brain yesterday?
Miss G—Somebody did.
How sad!—we always knew something would happen to those Sophomores.

Miss Crowe (during glee club practice)—"Ein Weh fasst mich!"

Mme. G.—Oh, Miss Crowe, you are very poetical.

Lillian McHenry, '13, has been elected exchange editor on the Sorosis board to fill the place left vacant by Marguerite Frey.

It has been suggested by a member of the Faculty that the Mandolin Club exchange their plebean instruments for harps and halos.

MUSIC NOTES.

The Mandolin Club gave a musical program at the Soho Settlement House, Thursday evening, March eleventh. The entertainment was in honor of Saint Patrick.

A recital was given Friday evening, March fourth, in Assembly Hall, by the advanced music students. Misses Susie Horner, Evelyn Crandall and Aurora Leedom were the pianists and Miss Mabel Crowe the organist. The Glee Club assisted in the program.

EXCHANGES.

The Buchtelite would be greatly improved by the addition of a literary department.

According to the Mercury, Gettysburg College was in a particularly thoughtful mood last month. The paper contained six articles of a serious nature. Among them, the "Ideals of Peace," and "America's Historical Rhine" are especially worthy of remark.

The Pharetra of Wilson College is among the best of our exchanges. It maintains an excellent literary department.

"What is geography?" asked the father who was testing his son's progress in study.

"Geography," replied little Jimmy Jiggs, "is what you put inside your trousers when you think you are going to get a whipping."

Follow your own shadow into the highway of success.

A Master-piece, Anyway—"Maud's hair is what you call Titian, isn't it?"

"Well, Titian or inni—Titian."

There are meters of accent
And meters of tone,
But the best of all meters
Is to meet her alone.

A New Proverb—No man is a hero to his own alarm-clock.

She—"How lovely of you to bring me those lovely roses and how fresh they are! I do believe there is a little dew on them yet."

He—"W-well, yes, there is; but I'll pay it tomorrow."

Hey diddle—diddle, the cat and the fiddle,
The cow jumped over the moon.
The Beef Trust laughed to see the rise,
And the citizen dined on a prune.

THE SOROSIS

VOL. XVI APRIL, 1910 No. 6

PATERNALISM.

Very often we hear the word "paternalism" used but not always with an accurate meaning. On the contrary, it is usually with a meaning that is both historically and philosophically incorrect. It carries with it a certain element of upperclass demagogism because generally used in the interest of the few as opposed to that of the many. When we speak of the management by the Federal government of telegraph lines and railroad systems, we are sure to hear the word paternalism used; it seems to designate any governmental activity. But we must remember that England does not regard the ownership and operation of a postal telegraph as paternalism, nor do the Germans call the street railways paternal in character. The truth, then, seems to be that paternalism has no reference whatever to the quantity of government functions but rather to the quality of these functions.

The theory was prominently advocated in England under the Stuarts and in France under the Bourbons, and there are still people who hold that "When there were only two people in the world, one was master. The following is an outline of a treatise written late in the seventeenth century, but which still finds supporters in our own day.

I. The first kings were fathers of families.

II. It is unnatural for the people to govern or choose governors.

III. Positive laws do not infringe the natural and fatherly power of kings.

It seems hardly possible that any man today, even with the greatest faith in the government, would accept such a theory, yet there are people that accept just that outline with word changes suitable to the present day. Paradoxical as it may seem we may have a paternal theory of the state, and at the same time advocate very limited functions of the state, or we may advocate very extensive functions going even to the extreme of socialism and yet adhere to the coöperative theory. There are, however, two kinds of socialism—paternal and fraternal, the latter seems to be too radical in that it has no respect for paternalism and reflects leadership and guidance from the superior class. For this very reason the German government has waged war against social democracy.

Granted that the coöperative theory of government is the correct one, it ought to include a certain element of paternalism. Democracies, to keep themselves strong and free from criticism, require the leadership of competent and strong men, above all other forms of government. In every country there is a large number of men who are virtually children and need a fostering care. In our own country we may take the negroes for example. Out of the institution of feudalism freedom grew merely as a negative. To men at that time, not to be restrained by the state meant freedom, while in our own time freedom implies participation in the activity of the state. There is a criticism that modern constitutional government is more expensive than the older absolute forms, but it is not more extravagant or more corrupt. Self-help is often opposed to the activity of the government but we should remember that self-help does not consist in making one's own bread, shoes and clothes, but rather in having things done for us and by our own agents. Those people who speak of governmental activity as paternalism have an un-American idea of the term.

There is a good deal of paternalism in the United States especially in the industrial field. It is claimed by private corporations performing public functions that the mass of the people is neither intelligent nor moral enough to perform them for themselves. Arguments to support it are the same worn out ones;—need of intelligence and integrity superior to the mass of the people. We all recognize the need of intelligence and integrity but we hold that those qualities should reside in the mass. Those who represent this modern industrial paternalism enjoy large revenues and let others labor, fight and die for them just as the old feudal lords did. Paternalism of a private character, notably among the rich, has made alarming progress and it is the kind that should be most strenuously resisted because it influences the poor to fold their hands and wait. We should feel encouraged to know that in many cases the evil is being resisted by the philanthropists themselves. One of the best examples is Mr. Carnegie. Before helping people he always inserts the clause, "provided you help yourselves." This is the only method by which each individual who reaps the benefits of the institution can be made to feel that he is a joint proprietor and has some responsibility. In the United States the state universities have grown much more rapidly than the private institutions. Berlin is now looked upon as the leading university of the world and all the endowments it has received from rich people amount to less than a million dollars. We as a people should be more self-reliant and practice self-help in all spheres of social life or this private paternalism in education will tend toward plutocracy. We may insist upon public support of public institutions and at the same time use private philanthropy.

There is a different side of paternalism which takes a dangerous form in legislation. "The higher type of man is not produced by the aid of a paternal government but by assurances of protection in his natural rights with encouragement to individual character." Governmental aid to the individual is not substantial but rather saps out his independence. Herbert Spencer says, "There seems no getting people to accept the truth which nevertheless is conspicuous enough that the welfare of a society and the justice of its arrangements are at bottom dependent on the characters of its members." It is said that "law is a progressibe science", therefore statutary enactments are necessary for the protection and safety of individuals. If carried to extreme it will dwarf the individual in his career of usefulness and we will have the degrading influences of a paternal government.

On the other hand statutes have been sustained regulating certain classes of business as manufacture and sale of intoxicating liquors, precautions in the use of dangerous machinery, safety and protection to the employes of the public. These are justified on the ground of increasing dangers and advancing civilization and the phrase "class legislation" no longer fills any one with apprehension. The aid of the state has often been sought and secured by corporations in the way of special and exclusive rights and to some extent the liberty of the individual has been limited. To meet this evil the recent constitution of Virginia provides that the general assembly shall not enact any "local, special or private law granting to any private corporation, association or individual any special or exclusive right, privilege, or immunity." Trusts seem to be a sort of defensive contrivance or a weapon used by property interests to defeat communistic attacks if we accept what a distinguished American author has said in discussing the origin of trusts. He explains them as follows, "Chief among the causes to be assigned for the present development of trusts is the recent communistic trend in the legislation of this country affecting corporations, or as one might say, aimed at corporations by both the State and the Federal legislatures.

Paternal legislation promises aid to the individual while, in reality it robs him of self-reliance and makes him the "ward of the nation." When the people are aroused they are stronger than any individual and all business combinations. In the Court of Appeals of New York one of the judges said, "Such governmental interferences disturb the normal adjustments of the social fabric and usually derange the delicate and complicated machinery of industry and cause a score of ills while attempting the removal of one." In Pennsylvania an act was passed "to secure operatives and laborers engaged in and about mines, manufactories of iron and steel and all other manufactories payment of their wages at regular intervals and in lawful money of the United States." The object was to prohibit the use of "store orders". The Supreme Court of Pennsylvania said this was an infringement alike of the rights of the employer and of the employe, an insulting attempt to put the laborer under a legislative tutelage which not only would degrade his manhood but would be subversive of his right as a citizen of the United States. Such legislation assumes that the employer is a tyrant and the laborer an imbecile. The result is to make an individual a mere hanger-on upon the government.

Paternalism keeps us from works of magnitude which would be a real blessing but does not prevent petty acts of interference. To go back to an historical review. "First the individual bears the burden; then the association of individuals; in the Middle Ages the Church, since the Reformation the state, that is, the people in their organic capacity takes up the work of civilization. We may say the ethical idea of the state is fraternalism, the state and the state alone stands for all of us."

THE SOUL OF A VIOLIN.

By Frances Alden Cameron, '11.

(Continued from last issue.)

Long, dreary months of suffering and terrible loneliness followed. The musician, crushed by his loss and worn out by the long weeks of hardship and strain, gradually aged into an old tired man. The light which went out from his eyes on the day his wife died never returned, but a deep yearning took its place, a yearning which grew so pitiful that strangers who passed him upon the busy streets turned to look again upon the sweet old face, with its patient mouth and saddened eyes, which some how appealed to them.

By degrees the wealthy banker who had purchased the violin from the musician came to feel an awakened interest in the old man and gradually drew out his story from his own lips. A puzzled expression came over his face at the mention of the child's name—"Cicely"—he repeated slowly, over and over again—"What a quaint, dear little name it is, a name which one does not often hear. Yet I have heard it before. Yes it was she—our Cicely"—springing up quickly from his chair, and rubbing his hands in his whimsical way, across his forehead and eyes.

"Cicely Everton was her name—a woman with the saddest story but the most beautiful character of any woman I have ever known."

A few weeks later, the musician received an urgent summons to go immediately south for a few weeks' visit with his new friend's relatives in Alabama, and to arrange for a long absence if possible—since his visit might be indefinitely prolonged.

"I am offering you a long rest here," he wrote in his kind yet whimsical way. "A rest, the ocean and the sound of your violin. I think you will admire the scenery about here—as well as my new home—Oak Place, which is considered quite a fine old mansion. I believe I am about to offer you also a most unusual test of your ability as a violinist—the musician's mystic power to call back a lost soul."

The letter reached the musician one winter evening as he sat alone in his attic rooms. He read the kind message through and looked up at the child's face on the wall—"Go," she smiled softly down at him through the twilight haze and the musician answered, "I will!"

Thurston met him in person at the little country station. He offered his hand in his cordial way to the old musician—and looking him straight in the eyes he said quietly—

"My dear friend, I am taking you home to your little girl." On the drive home he explained it all—telling as gently as he could the story of Cicely's past nineteen years.

"She married my cousin and that is how I have come to know her so well of late. He led her away from her father's home a child in years, a girl among thousands in beauty and character. They went immediately to Europe and from thence to the Orient, traveling continually for several years. He gave her all that his unlimited wealth and personal attraction could call happiness—and I think they were very happy for a short while. We never knew quite when or where it all ended but when he brought her back to us—seven years afterwards—she was a different woman. Her later years were very unhappy ones—and yet considering the man she married—I do not see how they could have been otherwise. He was not the man he should have been. And yet we were powerless to do anything—Cicely remained with him until the very last, bravest, sweetest, truest of all women I have ever known. Then came the accident—he died, we thought we must lose her—too, for a while,—she was so terribly injured. I am telling you all this because it is better that you should be prepared before you see her. Her mind is now completely gone. Her soul is as pure and beautiful as was the soul of the little girl who left you nineteen years ago. Yet she knows or remembers nothing of her past."

"Thank God," interrupted the old man suddenly, his eyes shining through their mists of unshed tears—"She is all mine now and no one else can have any claim about her. My own—my little girl. I am coming back to you!"

They came upon her in the summer house, sitting alone beside one of the rose wreathed windows, her hands folded idly within her lap—her eyes closed and her face resting wearily against the narrow window sill. She was a slender little thing, exquisitely framed but extremely frail. The face, which smiled up so sadly at them from its mist of soft, dark hair, bore indeed the look of the child who had gone away, aged with the years, but refined and sweetened by sorrow. She came forward to meet them in a childish, half frightened manner—while the musician, no longer able to restrain his passions of fatherly love, threw himself down at her feet and crushed both her hands to his lips. Thurston stole quietly away and left them alone together.

* * * * * * * * * * * * *

From the very first, there was absolutely no recognition on the part of Cicely for her father nor any remembrance of her past and earlier years. It was a great blow to the old man, yet he bore it bravely and tried to be content with having found his child again and by bestowing upon her all the pent up love and tenderness of the past years. She gradually came to have a deep feeling of affection toward the old man and an almost passionate regard for the violin, which sometimes he allowed her to play. She often admired the faded ribbon tied upon the old Cremona by her own childish fingers in the long ago yet with it came no memory of the day when she had placed it there—or indeed the mere fact that she had tied it on herself. She gradually became more and more listless regarding any past or future event, gradually lost all interest in even her personal surroundings, pleasures or friends, and day by day grew thinner, paler and more pensive, a slow withering away of a beautiful body, which had once enshrined a beautiful soul. Specialists of all description were summoned and each gave his verdict and hastened away. There was no hope. Absolutely no hope could be held out to the grief-stricken father and tenderly loving friend, unless in some way her soul could be called back again—by some voice or influence of her earlier years.

In the late summer they took her north again, quietly submissive, even smiling as the train rushed on past scenes so cruelly connected with the past sad years. When they arrived in New York four days afterward, a brighter colour seemed to shine in her usually pale cheeks a new radiance lighted her eyes—"Haven't I been here before—" she asked, and then intelligence faded—her mind went back to the dim silence as before.

* * * * * * * * * * * * *

At the musician's own request, they led her back to the old home—where for a while she seemed to grapple with the memory, so elusive of her past years. At last in desperation, the old man, sick at heart, yet even in his intense despair crying out to the wife of the long ago to come back as she had promised, in the hour of his greatest need, he led her up to the attic rooms, then silently knelt in prayer. The little girl on the wall smiled softly down on the child who had gone away, and the latter smiled back, without understanding why, yet seating herself as near as she could to where the child's portrait hung. It was twilight now in the attic rooms and nine months before on that very day, the mother's spirit had passed out into the great silence—leaving her promise behind. As though in the presence of some beautiful vision, too perfect, too celestial to be expressed other than by the divine agency of music, the musician rached out for his violin and softly began to play. And while he played—all the dim sweet memories of the long ago came back and wove themselves into his song, a song so full of tenderness and wistful pleading love that it was impossible to hear and not be deeply moved. Then through the midst of the beautiful melody, there rose and fell—one softly fingered strain, so soft, so exquisite, so ethereally beautiful in every way, that it was not akin to any music which the musician had ever heard before and he knew that but the impulse of it all—had sprung within his own heart. "You have indeed come back to me—heart's love," he whispered passionately to the violin, praying once more for the return of his child's soul. And it seemed to him that through the mists her mother's soul came back and offered up a prayer with his.

Cicely sat listening with folded hands and far away eyes, a puzzled, wondering look upon her beautiful face. But when the music changed and formed itself into a lullaby, one which she had often heard and loved as a very little girl, then she hesitated no longer, but arose in her childish half-timid manner and groped her way to her father's chair.

"I do not understand," she cried pitifully, lifting her face to his and scanning his face with tender yet troubled eyes.

"Where am I, father dear, and what has been happening all this while? I have slept—I think and dreamed such a strange sad dream! Then through it all—you seemed to call to me—and it was your voice which brought me back again—yours and my mother's too—"

"Your mother!" The words came involuntarily from the musician's lips. "Your mother's voice?" Then the woman smiled—the smile of the child in the golden frame, and the musician looked down into her love-lit eyes and realized that out of the mists her soul had indeed come back once more and it was to her as though she had never been away.

* * * * * * * * * * * * *

For a long while they sat before the fire in silence, the musician in his same old chair, and Cicely at his side, her head resting cosily against his arm as had often been their custom in the good old days gone by. She smiled as though she were indeed back in the girlhood she had never finished—and the musician played softly upon the old Cremona, and reverently also for he realized that to him had been granted a vision of the immortal and he had learned at last what is meant—by the Soul of a Violin.

SKETCHES

"ENGLISH AS SHE IS SPOKE."

As John Hartford wended his way disconsolately down Fifth avenue on the morning of February the twenty-second, when all the world was making holiday, he mentally cursed the business that could not allow him even that day to be spent with his wife and children at their home in the suburbs. The sign board of a prominent theater suddenly caught his eye. He knew that the play advertised was well worth seeing, and throwing all scruples against extravagance to the winds, went in and bought two of the best seats in the house for that evening's performance, and in his excitement recklessly failing to take account of the number of words, wired his wife: Have gotten tickets for theater this evening. Will meet you at 7.45 train. Supper afterward.

* * * * * * * * * * * *

"Well, of all things!" Mrs. Hartford exclaimed when she received her husband's telegram. "John must have had a big pull to have those tickets given to him. What good fortune!"

Mrs. Hartford hurried round to her friends and neighbors

and asked them to join the party. Mrs. Smith had intended going to a bridge-party, but sent her regrets rather than miss such an excellent play—with supper after it, too. Mrs. Ross did not care so much for the play, but she had a new silk gown that she was only too glad to have the chance of displaying. Mrs. Hartford had no trouble at all in collecting the merry company of ladies with a few gentlemen, nine in all, who boarded the 7:45 train for the city that evening.

When Hartford met his wife at the station, he thought it rather a strange coincidence that so many of his friends had come to the city that night also.

"O John, wasn't it perfectly splendid to get the tickets!" Mrs. Hartford gurgled happily as they started off, the rest of the company following.

"Well, I thought you deserved a treat for once, little mother, and so I blew myself."

"Why, John, you don't mean that you bought all those tickets, that they weren't given to you? I don't understand."

"Neither do I," John answered in complete bewilderment. But as he turned to survey the company, he felt a vague fear that he did understand. "What did that telegram say?" he demanded anxiously.

"It said you—why I believe I have it here in my satchel." And she pulled it forth. Hartford took it and read:

"Have got ten tickets for theater, etc." It was up to John.

Lillian McHenry, '13.

THEIR FIRST QUARREL.

She was five and he was six, and oh; but they were mad.

"I tell you," she cried angrily, "that six and seven is fourteen."

" 'Taint," he said, smiling cheerfully and serenely, "I know it's twelve."

"If it's twelve, Billy King, I'll never, ever speak to you again. You's a big story-teller, that's what you is," she finished triumphantly.

"Ruther be a story-teller than a girl," he said still smiling, but a little uneasy. "Anyway, I ain't."

"How dare you say you ain't when you is? Just go right home."

"I'll tell you what, Peggy. Here comes Sam. We'll ask him." And they both ran to meet the tall young man, coming up the walk. This was Sam, otherwise known as the uncle of Peggy.

"What's the fuss," he asked, as two panting children threw themselves bodily at him.

"She says it is, and it aint," Billy obligingly explained.

"I see," said Uncle Sam, "and he says it ain't, and it is—eh, Peggy?"

Two little heads nodded affirmatively.

"Who would like some candy," went on the one who understood.

"Me," they both shouted at once, and forgot their differences over a discussion of white and pink candy. While they were eating unrestrained, they explained their views on the sum of six and seven.

"I should think," said Uncle Sam, "that the safest way would be to split the difference, and call it thirteen."

Two sticky little faces were wreathed in smiles as they looked at each other.

"Why didn't we think of that before?" they said in chorus.

Alice Stoeltzing, '13.

A MONOLOGUE.

I thought I would wear this lavender gown tonight since the decorations are to be lavender and white—yes it is just a new one. I have never worn it before. Do you think so? I do too. So many people tell me lavender is becoming to my complexion. No, she did not make it? Miss O—, from S— made it for me. No, I never had her before, but I have made up my mind to have her again in the fall. Yes, very satisfactory—a little tight? I don't believe so, but is that hooked altogether right? Not hooked at all yet? Now that is all right —but it does feel rather strange. Too tight? No it certainly cannot be too tight, because she made it looser, but I could not stand it, and I insisted upon her making it tighter. I do hate to see a tight fitting dress hanging like a bag on a person. Oh yes, that is perfectly comfortable—only just unhook it there in that one place and put a pin in. There, that feels better. Does it seem to wrinkle there in front? Pull it down a little. Ah, there goes one of those hooks in the back. I did not expect you to jerk it like that—you were trying to get the wrinkles out? Well don't you know, I never have seen one of these tight-fitting dresses that did not wrinkle in front. Pulls so? Oh mercy no. That is just a small fold in the goods. Stouter than I used to be? No indeed, I weigh ten pounds less. One has to be moderately slim to wear one of these dresses becomingly. Why are you pulling it there under the arms? There goes another hook. Fix it? That's easy—just put a pin right there—that will hold it. Another hook pulled off? Oh, I did not mean to stretch so far round. You aren't supposed to play basketball in these dresses. Yes, the collar feels fine but I think I'll take out these stays at the side. They sort of jab my cheeks. There that's better. My collar crushed and pins all over? That doesn't matter. I shall wear my beautiful spangled scarf and my new lavender cape and no one will notice my collar or my pins.

Claire Colestock, '13.

"TAKING SUGGESTIONS."

Frazier was a sturdy lad of six years. John, who was two months older, was Frazier's chum. One morning the postman brought a letter to Frazier. He was overjoyed to receive it because a letter addressed to his very own self was a rare thing. As he opened it he thought how jealous John would be but his little heart beat very quickly and his head grew hot as he read the words written in an almost illegible hand—"Put twenty-five cents on the bak step b for toomorro or I'll shoot you." Directly below the last word was a poorly drawn black hand.

When he showed the letter to mother and pleaded for the necessary quarter, mother only laughed and went straight to the telephone. Four nine four-J," Yes, that was John's number.

Frazier listened breathlessly and this is what he heard. "Is this Mary? You just listen to your son's letter and then say that five cent theaters and nichelodeons do not have a bad influence on our children." As Frazier heard his mother repeat the words of his letter, he sighed, partly in relief, partly in sorrow at John's treachery. Martha Young, '13.

EARLY SPRING.

Early spring has come at last,
How glad we all should be;
For now we know that summer is near
When the buds and the blossoms we see.

The buds on all the trees come out
And look so pleased and smile
As if to say, "Now aren't you glad
We have come to stay awhile?"

Jeanne Gray, '13.

THE SOROSIS

Published Monthly by the Students of

Pennsylvania College for Women.

Subscriptions to the Sorosis 75 cents per year. Single copies 10c
Address all business communications to the Business Manager.
Entered in the Postoffice at Pittsburg, Pa., as second-class matter

Marlowe and Sothern played Romeo and Juliet a few weeks ago. My attempts to enter into the spirit of the play were seriously retarded by my neighbors. The woman behind me was remarking on the fact that Marlowe had grown too fat; and then wandered on to a discourse on her numerous admirers. She quieted down in time and my right hand neighbor attracted my attention. She was absorbed in the play but was evidently one of those people who cannot refrain from speaking their thoughts. "Aha, that's good, Aha," was kept up during the whole performance; and when Juliet drank the poison, she said, "Aha, she's going to drink it!"

There ought to be a law against talking in the theater, I thought. But my conscience began to hurt and checked my rising indignation. How many times had I been to lectures or concerts or plays and been bored? With glee I had exchanged withcisims with a friend unconscious of others. We have all done it. We all do it in our work and in our play, yet when our enjoyment is spoiled by another's thoughtlessness we feel righteously angered. It is just a matter of having a larger social consciousness, of realizing there are others to consider beside ourselves. If we could only remember, how many petty annoyances would be spared and perhaps a fairer attitude toward the leader or teacher or actor would increase our own enjoyment as well.

M. D. L.

COLLEGE NEWS.

The Freshman class gave a very successful performance of Miss Fearless and Company, Friday, March twenty-second. Invitations had been issued to the College and friends of the class and a large number was in attendance. The rehearsals were in charge of four members of the Junior class. The cast was as follows:

Miss Margaret Henley, an heiress............Martha Young
Miss Euphemia Young, her chaperon...........Grace Wilson
Miss Sarah Jane Lovejoy, from the Lost Nation...Helen Blair
Katie O'Connor, Miss Henley's servant......Bertha Richards

Miss Henley's guests...	
Bettie	Claire Colestock
Marion	Laila Clark
Peggy	Emma Geiselhart
Martha	Sylvia Wayne
Rebecca	Elizabeth McCague
Dorothy	Maude Shutt
Barbara	Esther Rosenbloom

"Just Lizzie," the ghost.......................Lucy Layman

Miss Alias }
Miss Alibi } "Silent Sisters"......... { Jean Gray
{ Elizabeth Donehoo

There was also music by the Mandolin Club.

Dr. Lindsay gave a very interesting talk on "Graft" Wednesday, April thirteenth. He explained the nature of graft and told some interesting incidents in connection with the graft trials now going on in Pittsburgh.

In spite of the snow, preparations have been progressing for May Day. May Day will be of an entirely different character this year, partaking more of the nature of the Old English Pageants and promises to be new and interesting.

The Easter service of the Y. W. C. A. was held in the Drawing Room of Berry Hall, Tuesday evening, March twenty-second.

Miss Coolidge entertained the South Hall girls and the Faculty at a pleasant little tea, Thursday afternoon, March twenty-fourth. In place of the usual Christmas sale the Y. W. C. A. held an Easter bazaar in the Drawing Rooms of Berry Hall. There was a splendid sale of Easter gifts, cards, posters and candy. The booth of the "Oriental" Fortune Teller was one of the main attractions.

Easter service was conducted in the chapel Friday morning, March twenty-fifth. Dr. Lindsay delivered the address and a quartette of Dilworth Hall and College girls furnished the musical part of the program.

On Wednesday morning, March thirtieth, the College and Dilworth Hall enjoyed an illustrated talk by Miss Hunter who showed in an interesting manner, with the aid of the blackboard, that the hands could be made render perfect obedience to the brain.

Thursday afternoon, April twenty-eighth, the newly organized German Club met in the Senior parlor. Miss Skilton, honorary member of the society, was present. Belle McClymonds, '11, and Florence Wilson, '11, were the hostesses and a pleasant afternoon was passed in guessing German riddles and playing "Deutche Dichety."

The "New Girls" of the house students entertained the "Old Girls" and the Faculty Friday evening, April fifteenth, with the "Biggest Show on Earth" in the gymnasium. Many daring and clever feats were performed to the astonishment of the audience, to say nothing of the "Great Minstrel Show" and the antics of the clowns.

Miss Bevere, a former member of our faculty, gave a pleasant talk in the library, Wednesday morning, April twentieth, on the work of Domestic Science in the University of Illinois. Miss Bevere has charge of that department of the university.

PERSONALS.

During the April vacation Mary Kramer, '10, entertained the Senior and Junior classes at her home in Perrysville avenue. The afternoon was passed in the pursuit of "Sweethearts" in which game prizes were received by Florence Wilson, '11, and Eva Cohen, '09, Frances Neel, '10, won a prize in a flower guessing contest. Dainty refreshments were served and the guests spent a most delightful afternoon.

Miss Ruth Peck has been very ill at the home of Miss Evelyn Crandall of Warren, Pa. Miss Peck spent the Easter vacation in Warren and has been unable to return to the College on account of her illness but her friends will be glad to know that her condition is much improved.

Miss Coolidge returned on Monday, eighteenth, after a very pleasant vacation spent at her home in Massachusetts and in visiting the large eastern colleges.

Miss Florence Bickel, Martha Sands, Mary Gray, and May Hardy have returned to the "Den" after spending the winter mouths in South Hall.

During vacation Miss Eleanor Davis visited her uncle, who is dean of Princeton Theological Seminary. She also enjoyed a short stay in New York.

Miss Virginia Siggins of Oil City, a former student of P. C. W., spent a few days at South Hall.

Mrs. J. C. Stahlmann of Vandergrift, Pa., visited her daughter, Calla, in South Hall March twenty-second.

Misses Evelyn Crandall and Calla Stahlmann spent Sunday, April seventeenth, with Miss Shinn of Carnegie.

Question:—"Whence the vivid illumination of the front piazza of South Hall, so newly acquired?"

Comedy in Logic.

Enter Junior at 8:35 to find a "little test" in progress, stares dazedly at questions on board, shakes head hopelessly and murmurs softly: "Innocence abroad."

Mabel Crowe, '11, has been chosen Queen of the May. The annual May Day exercises will take place on the campus May twenty-first.

Miss Ethel Tassey, '10 recently spent a few days with her sister at Markelton Sanatarium, Markelton, Pa.

MUSIC NOTES.

Master Dennis Chabot, the young Belgian pianist, gave a delightful informal recital in chapel, Wednesday morning, March twenty-third. Master Chabot has made arrangements to play with the London Orchestra next season.

The students of Madame Graziani and Mrs. Humphrey gave an informal recital in the Drawing Room, Thursday afternoon, March twenty-fourth.

The Glee and Mandolin Clubs are busily engaged preparing to fulfill their concert engagements. The home concert will be given May sixth, they will appear, one at Central Y. W. C. A., April twenty-ninth, and at Vandergrift, May thirteenth.

OMEGA NOTES.

The regular meeting of the Omega Society was held in the reception room Thursday afternoon, March thirty-first. After the business meeting, the following program was carried out:

Paper.................................Mary Hardy, '12
"Life of Robert Louis Stevenson"

Paper.................................Sara Carpenter, '11
"Treasure Island"

Paper.................................Irma Diescher, '11
"Master of Ballantrae"

EXCHANGES.

The Allegheny Monthly is full of excellent stories. "On the Santa Fe Freight" has an ingeniousness of plot and vividness of detail that is truly surprising in an amateur production.

The Lesbian Herald put out a good number last month, though for some reason, the exchange department was omitted.

The March number of the Washington-Jeffersonian was devoted to educational topics and was quite learned; as witness.

A Freshman thinks he knows it all,
A Sophomore knows he knows it all,
A Junior thinks he doesn't know anything,
A Senior knows he doesn't know anything.

We have never worn a Chanticleer Hat but we have played tennis in a duck suit. O, fowl pun.—Ex.

I rose up in a car one day
To give a girl my seat.
It was a question whether she or I
Should stand upon my feet.—Ex.

"What do you call it when you worship a debutante?"
"Buddhism."—Ex.

At the Postoffice—"Any mail for O'Leary?"
Clerk—"No."
"Oh, fudge."
Clerk (looking at file again)—"No, nothing for him either."—Ex.

At a dance—The Cuff—"Wilt thou?"
The Collar—"I wilt."—Ex.

Oily to bed and oily to rise
Is the lot of a man
When an auto he buys.
—Ex.

Teacher—"When did the 'Revival of Learning' begin?"
Student—"Before Exams."—Ex.

She—"Will there ever be a woman President?"
He—"No, the constitution says that the president must be over forty years old and a woman never gets that old."—Ex.

Be all you can,
Try all you can,
Do all you can—
and push.
—Ex.

THE SOROSIS

VOL. XVI MAY, 1910 No. 7

"ONLY MISS NELL."

The girl at the window laid her mandolin down very softly and turned away, her face still wistful with the spell of dreams.

"Miss Nell?" she felt her name called in a tired voice from a nearby cot where an aged soldier lay, with pain twisted face, awaiting the final call—"Wherenever—you—play—it—seems—as though—as though I were back in the old days again. She loved that song you know"—and the worn fingers clasped lovingly about the tiny miniature which lay against his breast. His wife's face, radiant with the beauty and charm of early womanhood, smiled tenderly up from the golden frame.

"I am glad," answered the nurse softly, caressing the old hero's hair—"If my music pleases you, for to each one of us of course, there is a long ago, which comes back in our dreams and in certain songs which we used to love."

"You are a Southerner?" queried the old soldier.

"Yes," the girl answered quietly. "My home was in old Kentucky, and that is why I love to play the dear old plantation songs so often." Then noting the lines of sorrow gathered about the old soldier's face—she cried impulsively. "And you long for it too. I saw it in your eyes, when first I began to play this afternoon. We are both from the South! Our dear brave courageous South land—" and through a mist of unshed tears, the girl, knelt and pressed her lips to the old warrior's scarred hand.

A few days afterward, a young officer, seriously wounded, was brought to this temporary hospital to be operated upon. From the very first, there was almost no hope of his recovery. Yet he seemed so young, so handsome, so full of courage and boyish hopes that a second operation was decided upon, with the slightest chance in the world of its proving a success. It did prove a partial success however and to Nell's especial care the young soldier was committed.

When she entered his room for the first time, he lay very quietly among the pillows, his brown curls loosened about his forehead and one slender ray of sunshine flickering across the brown hand outstretched upon the coverlet, and a tiny turquoise ring upon his little finger. The soldier's face lay almost in shadow, and a bandage was fastened across the eyes; but there was no mistaking the curve of the boyish lips and the ring she herself had given him, long ago, when both were children together. A sudden cry escaped the girl's lips.

"His name, sir?" she cried, turning to the surgeon at her side.

"Philip Wentworth—of the Tenth Regiment. Have you known him before, Miss Nell?" he asked suddenly, wondering at the sudden pallor on the girl's usually bright face.

"Hush, do not speak so loud," answered the nurse. "No —yes—I think I have met him—once—long ago; the name is familiar. Do not mention my name to him however—I am only Miss Nell—remember, only Miss Nell." A sudden mist gathered across the girl's eyes, and springing quickly forward she knelt beside the young officer's cot and laid her soft hand on his forehead. At the slight pressure he stirred, raised his unbandaged hand from the bed and groped dimly until he had caught Miss Nell's fingers.

"Is it you—oh Beatrice—you?" he whispered faintly. "Is —it you—at last?"

Thus he lay in delirium many days, with fast failing strength and no consciousness of the world about him, save when he called for water, catching the cool hands of Miss Nell in his own burning ones and crying in wistful tones, the name of the girl he loved. And the slender little lady at his side would bravely fight back the tears which had so often dimmed her brown eyes of late, striving to forget, meanwhile, the old memories which in spite of all her courage and ceaseless struggle often came back, to a heart which still suffered, but never flinched.

She had loved him so dearly in those old days, that the sweet remembrance of it all could never be quite forgotten. So during the cruel years of separation which followed, the thoughtless, passionate childhood had grown into a more subdued womanhool, refined, enobled, and humanized by the intense lessons which love and sorrow had taught. The lad had gone his way and forgotten—all but the fragrant memories of a Southern summer, and a goldenhaired child who had given him her ring and promised, always to wear and to cherish his. It had all happened nine summers ago. Philip still wore his ring, but Eleanor's was laid away in her treasure box, together with a faded flower a letter, and many pretty dreams which had never materialized. And now his keeping had been entrusted to her hands, and with the love for another woman glowing within his heart, he had come back to her for a little while—come back to her arms to die—to die!

Yet he would never know, must never know that the cool hands which so deftly arranged the bandages about his poor blinded eyes were the same dear hands he had often kissed in the far off Southland, that the voice whose music lulled him to sleep now in the long dark hours of pain and suffering, was the same one to which he had never listened without a thrill in those other days—nor that the little girl whom he had once loved still cared for him and always would care—until the end. To him as to the others she would be known simply as Miss Nell.

By degrees the delirium lessened, and one afternoon Philip told Eleanor of the woman he loved—her name being one which the girl had frequently read in the social journals of the day, for her personal beauty and the social position of her family.

They had evidently been engaged for several years and were to be married as soon as the war came to an end. He loved her with a devotion which seemed almost akin to worship, and could scarcely wait for the letter he felt sure she would send at the first knowledge of his illness. But as day after day passed and no letter came—Eleanor saw strange lines of anxiety creep into the soldier's face and she knew that his disappointment was very keen. Gradually, his remaining strength lessened, and at last there came a day when even the girl herself, she who had hoped and fought and prayed the longest for the soldier's life, was forced to admit the coming of the end. At length in desperation, driven almost to madness by the anguish within her heart, and scorn of the thoughtless girl who could dance and enjoy life so thoroughly while her lover lay dying in a city hospital, Nell herself, wrote a telegram to Phil's sweetheart; urging, beseeching her to come —or at least send—her farewell.

"If she truly loves him," thought the broken-hearted girl, "she will come to him at once, and there will be no need of a reply."

* * * * * * * * * * *

But the next day passed and the one following, and still there came no word.

"She does not care, she will not heed, and he will die," cried Nell at last in utter despair, leaving the ward to fight out alone the great sorrow which for a while longer must be borne without an outward sign. When she returned to the sick room, there was a brave smile on her lips and a new light in her eyes, eyes so tender, radiant and beautiful, that the glory of her presence seemed to brighten the little room with an unseen charm. Kneeling softly beside the soldier's cot, she whispered in his ear, very gently and clearly, the name of Beatrice. He stirred suddenly—and answered to the beloved name.

"You have heard from her? She is coming, my own, at last?" And the girl answered.

"Yes, she loves you, more than she has ever loved you before this time. She will be here, tomorrow, and here is the letter. I leave it here—in your hand—through the night."

She laid it softly in the soldier's hand and turned away. A great peace stole gradually over the lad's tired face, and he sank to sleep with the forged letter held close to his lips. Yet long into the dark silent hours of the night, a white robed girl sat with folded hands and eyes that looked back into a distant summer, the fragrance of whose memory came back again as the perfume of a faded flower, will often breathe forth again some subtle reminder of its former charm, though hidden away perhaps in the silence of many years. She sat so near to the sleeping man that with one movement of her arm, she could reach out and caress the brown hair or the thin hand upon which rested her own ring, and she recalled with wistful pleasure the moment when he had caressed the pretty trinket in her presence and said:

"I wear it for a memory." She had wondered at the time to what memory he referred, yet never since then had the courage come to refer to the matter again. Her heart gladdened at the faint smile which came over her hero's face—and—"It is I who love him the more," she murmured softly to herself. "And it is because of my love that he sleeps and dreams, of her—! And yet, he is worth—the lie!"

At dawn he awoke once more, but with the awakening passed again into the delirium, which never left him until the end. He called constantly for Beatrice, and toward the last seemed to regard Nell herself as the woman he loved. At the very end, she took her mandolin and sang softly to her own accompaniment—the song which as a child he had always loved—"My Old Kentucky Home." A smile passed over his face and he held out his arms with a passionate gesture toward the singer at his side.

"Come, sweetheart," he called. "You are Beatrice, are you not?" he said anxiously, groping with his tired hand for the girl's face. And Nell at last hesitated no longer. With all the pent up love and tenderness, which so long she had forced herself to conceal, shining forth from her dark eyes and glorifying her girlish face, she came swiftly over to where the soldier lay, gathered him close in her strong young arms and rested her lips on his.

"It is I, Phil—I who have come to you at last."

* * * * * * * * * * *

A few days after the funeral of young Wentworth, there came to the hospital a letter addressed to Miss Nell, and bearing the postmark Cincinnati. Within lay simply a card announcing the engagement of Miss Beatrice Farrell to a young lawyer of the same city. Underneath it, was scrawled in a dashing yet girlish hand: "Explain to him, if you can; but no doubt you will readily understand why I am not in a position to attend Philip Wentworth under the present circumstances."

It was signed merely with the initials "B. F." and a delicate odour of sandalwood arose from the envelope and pervaded the atmosphere of the room.

Outside her window, a band of wandering musicians, were playing several of the old fashioned Southern melodies which she had so greatly loved, and as they passed onward down the street, the last bars of "My Old Kentucky Home" floated in at the opened blinds, and loosened at last the floodgates of tears, which so long she had held tightly closed.

"No, dear heart," she whispered, almost revently to herself—repeating the closing refrain. "For you and me there will never be a goodnight that can last. This is but our beginning and eternity holds the end."

Frances Alden Cameron, '11.

BROWNING'S POEMS TO HIS WIFE.

It is impossible to read the poems which Browning has written to his wife or in which he refers to her without getting a wonderful idea of their relation to each other. She was the inspiration of life. In many ways the love of Robert Browning for Elizabeth Barrett was a revival and renewal of the condition of tenderness and sympathy that existed between Browning and his mother. There certainly was a strongly marked resemblance in the characters of the two women. To many people this accounts for the instant affection that Browning felt toward the occupant of the darkened room when first they met.

On account of the singular perfection of his married life, he was qualified to understand the comradeship possible between a man and a woman where the two natures are alike and mutual respect and comprehension can join forces with depth of feeling. Tennyson was fond of discussing the "woman problem." Browning never did so. He substituted for Tennyson's abstract theories an ardent impression of the joy of living when heart and brain are dedicated worthily to one great affection. Love as the eternal union of two souls finds expression again and again in his poems. Love is the guardian angel of the soul on its way toward the higher life. Browning's poems form a lover's litany to that elect few who hold that the true meeting of a man and a woman is the marriage of the mind.

"Men and Women," the first volume published after his marriage, shows how much love was to him and how it had enlarged rather than lessened his conception of romantic affection. Especially in the dedicatory poem to his wife, "One Word More," considered by many critics as the sweetest and loftiest of all his poems, does he express his deep feeling.

Take them, Love, the book and me together
Where the heart lies, let the brain lie also.

He turns to Dante and Raphael for inspiration with which to address his wife. They drew on their imaginations for the women they painted, having the help of real women, it is true; Browning has not found it necessary to go from his own fireside to find the Madonna of Raphael or the angel of Dante. In his poem he says:

God be thanked, the meanest of his creatures
Boasts two soul-sides, one to face the world with
One to show a woman when he loves her!

Into the poem "By the Fireside," Browning has put a strong accent of personal feeling. He has expressed his ideal of womanhood as he knew it through the one who was "dearest and greatest and best" to him in life as in genius. It shows us simple domestic affection as a help to man and woman in the home. It leads to growth of soul. The lover has found that life is a means of discovering himself to himself, testing his own capacities and showing others what he can be to them. In this process of self-revelation nothing is so important as love which searches into every corner of the soul and brings out everything there is in one.

The permanence of this affection, woven of many threads of intellectual and emotional correspondence is shown by poems written after the death of Mrs. Browning. It was three years after this took place before he wrote "Prospice" ending in a passionate expression of his belief in immorality.

"O thou soul of my soul! I shall clasp thee again,
And with God be the rest."

Seven years later he recorded his undiminished sense of loss in the introduction to "The Ring and the Book."

"Never may I commence my song, my due
To God who best taught song by gift of thee,
Except with bent head and beseeching hand—
That still, despite the distance and the dark,
What was, again may be; some interchange
Of grace, some splendour once they very thought,
Some benediction anciently they smile."

His love lived on with growing depths of yearning and reality, because it was not merely a love to the person but a love for the soul; it was a union of heart with heart in what is spiritual and therefore eternal.

Sarah R. Carpenter, '11.

SKETCHES

MARK TWAIN.

No longer has America a great humorist, for Mark Twain has gone from among us and there seems to be no one capable of taking his place. Bor n in a rough little Western mining town he came to be an author of world wide fame. Mark Twain is known most widely as a humorist, "the man who makes us laugh," and while all who knew him knew that his laughter was clean and wholesome, that he scorned the empty vanities and pretensions of the world, few realized the sterling qualities of the man. He was a man of sadness and when he provoked us to our greatest laughter his heart was often sore. He was a man of great personal honor and reminds us of Scott in his assumption for honor's sake of debts for which he was not legally liable. He is one of the best known of American authors abroad and was honored with many foreign degrees. But through all he remained plain and unassuming. He will live in our memories as our greatest humorist and an ideal American! Sarah Stuckslager, '13.

THE OLD STONE HUT.

The small stone dwelling had but one room, of moderate size, with a great chimney. Between the chimney and the eastern wall was a couch, which also served for a bed. The western side was given over to a few well-polished kitchen utensils, a churn and a bread trough. The floor was of earth, but a strip of home-made carpet was laid down before the fireplace. There was also a table, a spinning wheel, and a shelf of books. It was not the hut of a fisherman, though upon the wall opposite the books there hung fishing tackle, nets and cords. Upon two shelves were arranged carpenters' tools, polished and in good order. Everywhere there were signs of a man's handicraft as well as of a woman's work. Apart from the tools there was no sign of a man's presence in the hut, but whatever was the trade of the occupant, the tastes were above those of the ordinary dweller. A gold-handled sword hung above a huge, well-craved oak chair. The chair relieved the room of anything like commonness and somehow was in accord with the simple surroundings. It was clear that only a woman could have so perfectly arranged this room. After visiting this hut we mountain-climbers wandered on our way, no wiser as to its owner than before we entered it.

Esther A. O'Neil, '13.

A GAME OF BRIDGE

Scene: A parlor, four seated at a table playing cards. One does near all the talking.

Well, I do hope that I dealt myself a good hand this time—last time I dealt? Why, no I don't think that was a very good hand, why I never—Oh is it my bid? Well, let me see, (counts cards) I could make it—no I think I'll —Oh I'm going to bridge it this time. As I was saying I never dealt myself a good hand in my life. Have you seen Mrs. Smith's new hat? She had it on Sunday, and it's a perfect fright. I wouldn't—Is it my turn? Who played that ace? You did? I wouldn't wear it to a dog fight. Dear me, what did you say is trump? You see, I have so much on my mind, worrying about the house and the children that I can't remember at all. Oh yes, hearts, sure enough. I must try to remember. The children are always so restless late in the afternoon, that I always feel fidgety about them when I'm away, although I don't when I'm at home, I have such a—is it my lead? I have such a fine nurse for them, but it always looks well for a woman to—of course I led the wrong card, and that gives you the odd, doesn't it? and finishes the rubber.

Margaret Minor, '13

NEXT TO NOTHING.

One morning the new cook came to Mrs. West and said she could not use the kind of flour which was in the bins. She had always used one kind and would not use any other. Mrs. West asked her what the name of this special kind was and the cook replied "Next to Nothing." Mrs. West said that while she was rather dubious about getting a flour with such a name she would try to obtain it. She telephoned the grocer about it and he said he had never heard of such a flour but would try to procure it for Mrs. West. In a short time he called up saying that there was no such flour on the market, but there was one called "Second to None." Mrs. West asked the cook if she did not mean that and the cook replied "Oh yes, I knowed it was something like that."

Lucy Layman, '13.

ANECDOTE.

There was once a little boy about five years old who was always kept very closely at home with his mother and father and grandmother. His grandmother had been in poor health for some time and people would keep asking him how she was. He would always answer that she was not very well. One day his aunt asked him how his grandmother was, and, after thinking quite a long time and evidently trying to remember a phrase he had heard his mother say he answered, "I don't know just how she is now, but they say she is worn to the thread-bone."

Louise Fletcher, '13.

THE SOROSIS

Published Monthly by the Students of

Pennsylvania College for Women.

Ethel Tassey, '10 .... Editor-in-Chief
Elma McKibben, 10 .... Business Manager
Minerva Hamilton, '11 .... Literary Editor
Elvira Estep, '12 .... College Notes
Calla Stahlman, '12 .... Personals
Lillian McHenry, '13 .... Exchanges
Gertrude Wayne, '11 .... Assistant Business Manager

Subscriptions to the Sorosis 75 cents per year. Single copies 10c
Address all business communications to the Business Manager.
Entered in the Postoffice at Pittsburg, Pa., as second-class matter

FREEDOM OF THE PRESS.

During President Taft's recent visit to Pittsburgh an incident took place which might be used to good advantage by those opposed to the twentieth century "Freedom of the Press". Many such things occur every day, but this was brought home to us with force, being a direct attack upon the character of the students of Pennsylvania College for Women.

As most people do not know (thanks to the newspapers) an arrangement was made by Dr. Lindsay with the assistance of Mrs. T. M. Laughlin by which the school was to adjourn to the Laughlin lawn and hear a short speech from Mr. Taft. It probably would have been pretty tame for a reporter to note that the girls, with Dr. Lindsay at their head, marched two by two to the Laughlin place and there arranged themselves in an orderly manner to await the President. It would have sounded pretty common place to say that three hundred school girls received the President and his speech with enthusiastic applause and at a respectful distance.

Oh, it put so much life into the affair and made it more "Just Like You Read About" in books on boarding-school escapades to represent the girls as a mob of gushing school-girls bent on "Hobsonizing" the President. It sounded more realistic to have them sing a jargon of "Hurrah for Bill" rather than a college song; and to yell, "I love my Pennsylvania College, but oh, you big Bill Taft." The President received so much applause elsewhere that it introduced a little variety and also was quite appropriate to have his remarks punctuated in this case with "Giggles"—"Coughs"—"Titters Galore."

No doubt those who began the struggle for "Freedom of the Press" were actuated by a sincere and lofty purpose. The idea was probably farthest from their minds that it would procure for them the right to represent the proper action of a well-behaved assembly of young ladies as an act of violence committed by a mob of rowdies. This is the actual extent to which this "Freedom" has gone. No person or institution is any longer safe from a like misrepresentation. It would certainly seem as if the limit had been reached.

The following from the "Louisville Herald" seems appropriate:

The Newspaper Guy.

I find a man pushing his way through the lines
Of the cops where the work of the fire fiend shines.
"The chief! I inquire—but a fireman replies:
"Oh, no; why, that's one of those newspaper guys."

I see a man walk through the door of a show,
Where great throngs are blocked by the sign, "S. R. O."
"Is this man the star that no tickets he buys?"
"Star nothin'! He's one of those newspaper guys."

I see a man start on the trail of a crook,
And he scorns the police, but he brings him to book,
"Sherlock Holmes!" I inquire—someone scornfully cries:
"Sherlock Holmes h—l! Naw; that's one of those newspaper guys."

And some day I'll pass by the great Gates of Gold
And see a man pace through unquestioned and bold
"A saint?" I'll ask, and old Peter'll reply:
"No; he carries a pass—he's a newspaper guy."

ALUMNÆ.

Friday, May 13th, Mr. Charles H. Caffin, the well known art critic, delivered the first lecture that has been heard at the College for some time. Dilworth Hall was crowded with an appreciative audience of students, faculty and alumnae. Mr. Caffin won special admiration by his ability to present in such a simple manner a subject so obviously deep as "The Relation of Realism and Idealism in Art." One did not need to be a student of art to follow him. From time to time during the last three years the College has been indebted to the alumnae for some very good lectures but this one has exceeded them all.

Miss Irma Beard has returned home after teaching for a term in the High School at Stoneborough, Pa.

Miss Edna McKee and Miss Clara Niebaum enjoyed the College Musical Club concert at Vandergrift, Pa.

The friends of Miss Grace Stevenson will be glad to know that she has recovered from the effects of her accident.

Died—Mr. W. A. Edeburn, father of Miss Edith Edeburn, '96.

Four of the children in the May Queen's train are "Alumnae Babies". They are Jane Duff Philips, Eleanor Bard Fulton, Elizabeth Bryant Stevenson, and Thomas Hanna.

Pittsburg Press)

t addressing the Students of Pennsylvania College for Women. On his left
Dr. H ,D. Lindsay, President of the College.

Pittsburg Press.)

COLLEGE NEWS.

When President Taft visited Pittsburgh on Monday May second, we were all glad to accept an invitation to meet him at the residence of his sister, Mrs. Thomas K. Laughlin, in Woodland Road. About ten o'clock in the morning, the students assembled upon the lawn before Mrs. Laughlin's home. Mr. Taft and his escort soon appeared and after the singing of "The Purple and the White" and "Dilworth Hall," he addressed his audience as follows:

"You are indebted to me for this opportunity to come out here this morning and get away from your studies. I trust that if I make no other impression upon you, for this reason if for no other, I will win your gratitude. I congratulate you on being educated under such charming surroundings. I know that you will go on and on and that you are destined to play an important part in the life of this great nation—whether you vote or not."

Dr. Kane gave a very interesting twenty minute talk in Chapel May eleventh, on Siam, where he has been a physician for years.

Wednesday morning, May eighteenth, Dr. Lindsay spoke on the subject of "Peace and Peace Conferences."

College girls are busy preparing schedules for next year.

A number of pictures were taken by a representative from the Ladies' Home Journal, May sixth, for publication next fall. Among the groups were selected the Musical Club and next year's Seniors in cap and grown, and a scene from the Senior play, "The Romancers."

PERSONALS.

Sincerest sympathy is extended to Miss Mary Keen, '13, in the loss of her father, Mr. B. F. Keen, who died Wednesday morning, May eighteenth.

Mrs. Coolidge has been living at the college since Easter vacation.

Miss Kerst was very ill for a few days during the second week of May.

Miss B.—Many Christians met death at the hands of wild beasts.

Miss Hickson (in Chemistry)—When sun acts on HgCl it breaks it down and causes salvation.

Miss B. (to Miss T.)—What is the difference between a prophet and a preacher?

Miss T.—A preacher preaches all the time (Laugh). I mean he always says the same thing.

The Vandergrift contingency of South Hall entertained a number of members of the visiting Musical Club after the concert in Vandergrift. With Mrs. Armstrong at Vandergrift Heights were Miss Coolidge, Miss Kathan, Miss Mabel Crowe, Miss Florence Wilson, Miss Maude Demmler, Miss Elma McKibben and Miss Ethel Tassey. With Miss Calla Stahlman were Misses Amelia Horst, Anna Larimer, Alice Darrah and Evelyn Crandall. With Miss Martha Young, Misses Ionia Smith, Louise Fletcher, Claire Colestock, Margaret Titzel and Maude Shutt. With Miss Vivian Stitt, Misses Florence Bickel and Martha Sands, With Miss Spiher, Miss Lillian McHenry.

A number of South Hall girls attended a dance given by the Washington and Jefferson Glee Club following its concert in the Conservatory of Music, April twenty-eighth. Mrs. Armstrong and Miss Kathan chaperoned the affair.

Lieutenant Peary recently made a proposal to deliver an address in Ann Arbor, but was refused. The Michigan Daily says, "The commitee in charge are satisfied that Dr. Frederick Cook furnished enough Artic dope here for one year."

A course in college songs is being given this year at the University of California. A similar course would be by no means useless at other schools that might be mentioned.

He (after half an hour's hard work)—"You didn't know that I danced, did you?"

She—"No. Do you?"—Ex.

Wise-looking Freshman (entering Dean's office)—"Is the Dean in?"

Clerk—"No."

Freshman—"When will he be in?"

Clerk—"I can't tell you. Is there anything I can do for you?"

Freshman—"No, I only wanted to get a catalogue."—Ex.

"The carriage waits without, my lord."
  "Without what, gentle sir?"
"Without the left-hand running board,
  Without the French chauffeur,
Without a drop of gasoline,
  Six nuts, the can of oil,
Four pinions, and the limousine,
  The spark plug and the coil,
Without the brake, the horn, the clutch,
  Without the running gear,
One cylinder—it beats the Dutch
  How much there isn't here!
The car has been repaired, in fact,
  And you should be right glad
To find that this much is intact
  Of what your lordship had.
The garage sent it back, my lord,
  In perfect shape throughout;
So you will understand, my lord,
  Your carriage waits without."—Ex.

CONTENTS

Spahr & Ritscher, Printers, 6117 Kirkwood St.

THE SOROSIS

VOL. XVI JUNE, 1910 No. 8

THE SWORD OF THE SAMURAI.

The first clear memory that the little Toro had of his childhood was when they brought home his father's blood-stained sword and told his mother that her hero had been of service to his country and—had kept the faith. So the little fellow had realized then that the gay, pleasure loving young father would never come back to them again; and that he must grow up as strong and brave to protect the frail little mother as his father would have wished and above all to honour the spirits of his departed ancestors and remember that he was the son of a Samurai, he to whom had been intrusted a hero's sword and memory.

He had grown up into boyhood under the shadow of the sword, whose hilt was chased with beaten gold and upon whose blood-stained blade were engraved the words "Son of a Samurai, the country has need of thee." Toro remembered so well how big and brave he had felt when for the first time he had been permitted to flourish the sword in his hand, and promised his mother that some day he would go to battle and promote the glory of the family name. A sudden swift radiance had overspread his face and springing suddenly forward she had caught the child in her arms and laid her face upon the blade as though it were a living thing.

"Oh little son," she whispered radiantly, smiling up into the child's bright face—"You are a hero's son—and a hero's spirit is shining in your eyes. So take the sword now, little son. Henceforth it is thy very own—and in your keeping lies its future glory."

* * * * * * * * * *

A few years afterward. Toro left the sunrise country for the land beyond the ocean—America, to which many years before, his own father had gone and received his education at one of the oldest universities in the United States. It had been his mother's desire that her son should grow up after the fashion of his father, so stifling the many heartaches and the intense dread of the loneliness which she knew would follow his departure, she sent him away with all the prayers and hopes and wistful tenderness a mother's heart can understand. He wrote her very frequently, bright, manly letters of the life and interests in the strange new country to which he had gone, full of tender messages to herself, quaint allusions to his natural stupidity in acquiring the new customs and language and always at the end—"I remember the Samurai trust," which gladdened the heart of Yuki, and caused her to pay more frequent visits to the shrines of the Shokonska, where she might receive blessings for herself and the son who was true to his country although in another land. So for his sake and partly to while away the long hours of loneliness and monotony during her son's absence, she made the acquaintance of an English missionary at Tokyo, and by degress came to acquire a slight familiarity with the English language, the mannerisms of the people and above all the Christian beliefs and religion. "I shall not tell him until he returns," she thought happily to herself. "It will be a surprise and how pleased and proud he will be to find that I can share his knowledge of the foreign land and people." Shortly afterwards she received a letter from Toro which fille her heart with a strange new dread.

"I love—oh mother mine," he wrote in the boyish impetuous way which she loved so well, "I love an American girl—and it is so glorious to write and tell you that I am loved in return. She is so young—and so beautiful!—a slender little lady, all fire and sunshine and dew—and her eyes, they are dark like yours but her hair, it is like gold in the sunlight and ripples like the waves in our brooklet at home."

A photograph was enclosed and revealed a young, girlish face with tender eyes and a strange, foreign beauty, full of character and youthful charm. The brown eyes met the gaze of Yuki with a wistful appeal, which stirred the older woman's heart.

"He loves—her—the daughter of a foreigner," she whispered faintly striving to still the jealous protest of her heart. "I wonder whether he will marry and forget in his love for her—the glory of his father's name and the trust of the Samurai sword—No! no, that cannot be," she cried,"he has remembered it still, he will not forget that the blood of a hero runs in his veins. Surely I was wrong in doubting my son."

So she turned to her letter once more and read on to the very last word, but although it was filled with tender messages to herself and his great eagerness to return and see the clear homeland which he had not witnessed for so many years, there was no mention of the Samurai sword. It was the first time that the oft repeated phrase, which meant so much to her mother heart, had been neglected—or forgotten, and with a sudden cry she hurled the photograph aside, as though its very presence, symbolized the changed devotions of her son.

* * * * * * * * * *

He returned to Japan in the early summer and through a mist of falling blossoms his mother stood at the threshold of their tiny home to welcome him, her face aglow with wistful happiness.

"My son!" she cried joyously—"My son, returned to me at last." Then gazing long and earnestly into the dark eyes overhead she cried reverently, sinking to her knees in the manner of her people—"Son of Samurai and worthy to bear the name!" He answered her words with a smile and Yuki realized that his mind did not linger long upon what she had just said.

* * * * * * * * * *

They were to be married the following fall. By degrees, Yuki began to feel a new interest in the golden haired girl across the seas and a strange though at times jealous delight in the prospect of having a daughter, whether foreign or not, her race might be. Often times, she enclosed quaint tender little messages in her son's letters, which were replied to at once in the bright impulsive manner of the American girl who longed to know and love the little lady in Japan for her own sake as well as her lover's.

Rumors of war, meanwhile had been circulating all summer and by September it had become an established fact. Anxious lines began to creep into Yuki's wistful face whenever she looked at her son; but he, boylike, gave no marked attention to aught save his preparations for marriage. He had planned to leave the first of October for the United States and the following December planned to return to Japan with his bride. They hoped in time to be able to persuade Yuki to come back to America and make her home with them.

One morning at daybreak, Toro awoke to find his mother missing from her room. The soft futons, upon which she was accustomed to sleep, were undisturbed, and the light still burned before his father's shrine. He stole quietly to the living room door and found her there. Outstretched upon the matted floor she lay, and fast asleep, as though completely worn by suffering or pain. An open letter was in her hand, and close to her heart was clasped her husband's sword. Her face was very pale and bore marks of the long, sleepless night she had passed. Unconsciousness had come only after hours of pain and mental anguish, which she had borne in silence. Toro at once reached the slender figure and gathered her up tenderly in his arms. She opened her eyes—half dazed and after a moment's hesitation, deep worry within her gaze, gave the letter to Toro to read. He grasped the contents at a glance but his face paled. It was very brief, but the tone was imperative, a summons for him to report at the headquarters of the war department, the following week, in charge of a regiment, with which he had been trained, years before, in military school. His boyhood companions remembering his former military ability had themselves asked for him as their commander and through them he felt the call of his country, his people and the spirit of those who had died and gloried in so doing, for the name and honour of their Japan.

"Mother," the boy answered gravely, drawing her head down to his shoulder and looking into her great dark eyes—"I am going out into the garden alone, to think awhile. Pray for me that I may be guided aright, that I may be true to her and to my country—as well."

He left her then and passed out into the garden, bright and beautiful with the rosy glow of dawn, down through the garden path, to the groves of cherry trees, and the river side.

Beyond through a mist of rosy clouds, the silver cone of Fuji Yama, gleaned brightly in the early sunshine. It was the coming of a new day, and the wonder, the mystery of it all amazed the lad, with its marvelous splendor and beauty. The spirit of the morning passed into the boy's soul.

He drew out Margaret's picture from its silver case and gazed long and deeply into the beautiful face. The dark eyes never wavered in their gaze from his, and the red lips were curved into a smile. He had never before quite so clearly realized how wonderfully lovely she was, his Margaret, his own little sweet heart across the seas. A letter lay enclosed within the case. It breathed of violets, the fragrance which he always associated with her, and while he read, a great tenderness stole over his face. She was so young and he loved her so!

The garden, the river, the sunshine, all faded from his sight and he saw only a slender girl looking up earnestly into his face and promising to leave her people and follow him into another land. The vision merged into another and he saw his mother, in all her girlish beauty and slenderness, lying upon the Samurai sword, and all the love, the sadness upon her tired face. "Son of a Samurai, thy country has need of thee." The words burned themselves into his brain, but he could see only the long years which lay ahead, wherein his frail mother must live on alone, without the support of either husband or son, whose names were now enrolled in the glory of Japan's memory. The wife, the mother of the Samurai! He thought once more of the girl across the sea who waited for his return.

Then he returned and looked up once more at the distant mountain, under whose shadow his father, like himself, had grown up into manhood and given his life for Japan. For a long while he continued to gaze toward the west and gradually his face became quite calm and clear. He turned to greet his mother with a smile upon his lips, saying no word, but taking her tenderly within his embrace, and holding her so for a long while. The violet fragrance of Margaret's letter mingled strangely with the odor of cherry blossoms, which Yuki always wore in her dark hair.

Frances A. Cameron, '11.

TENNYSON AND BROWNING.

In comparing two such potent literary forces of the nineteenth century as Tennyson and Browning we are indeed treading upon dangerous ground. For each has won his way into our hearts, and established himself there, by a totally different method.

Tennyson appeals first by his art; the music of his style and the simplicity of his treatment. After this, or rather by means of this, one is drawn to his philosophy and the breadth of his ideals. Browning impresses us first with his message. After that we think of the admirable vehicle he used to convey it. In philosophy, these poets have divided between them remarkably the movements of manhood spirit.

The differences of style of the two men are numerous, in fact the two have practically nothing in common. Tennyson put first the melody and music of what he wrote to attract the thought. Browning put thought first—and was concerned principally with what he said, not how he said it. Consequently the smooth fluent style of Tennyson has made him famous, while the roughness of Browning frequently detracts attention, where the subject matter is well worth notice. Tennyson's art was undoubtedly studied, to enhance the thought. But just as truly was Browning's apparent lack of it, studied. It was his own wish to appeal to the class of thinkers, while it was Tennyson's desire to attract all, to make everyone think, and at the same time to give pleasure. Tennyson is generally known as the artist, for his philosophy has never received just appreciation. Browning has been called the philosopher, and just as unjustly his art has been ignored.

The two men are both lasting spiritual forces. Tennyson speaks to us more often in his own person, than Browning.

The latter speaks through the personalities of many. Rarely does he show us himself as himself. Tennyson's moral teaching is special, and realistic. He began by taking Christ as a certainty, believed in without proof. Browning led up to his supreme belief in Christ. Neither is bound by any set religious law. Religion was to Tennyson, faith in immortality. To Browning, it meant supreme overwhelming joy in the Divine presence. His teachings are ideal, and philosophical.

Their different attitudes toward death are admirably shown in the two death poems, Tennyson's "Crossing the Bar", and Browning's "Prospice". Browning dwells more upon the growth of the soul in this world; and the remoteness and small consequence of death. Tennyson treats of it as a near and tangible thing, as the consummation of this life. He dwells upon the hope of immortality and of the future life.

"I hope to meet my pilot face to face
When I have crossed the bar."

The nature poems of Tennyson are more plentiful than those of Browning. Tennyson, for the mere love of description at which he was an artist, added many a line or stanza which was not necessary to the thought, but merely added beauty. Browning spared everything which he considered foreign to the thought. He nowhere attempts portrait painting, but often gives us a complete picture by only two or three touches. He was primarily the student of human nature, and was so engrossed with it that he had no time left for nature study.

The different ideas of the poets are brought out more clearly by a comparison of Tennyson's "In Memoriam" and Browning's "Saul." In Saul, we see Browning, as always, the poet of the individual initiative, and the supreme moment. Love is discussed in both these poems from the different view points of the poets. Tennyson portrays it as it makes itself felt through bereavement, making it typical and universal. In thought, it carries ennobling love from the individual to the social, until he is able to say,

"Strange friend, past, present, and to be
  Loved deeplier, darklier understood;
Behold I dream a dream of good,
  And mingle all the world with thee."

Browning's Saul portrays the highly favored individual finding his highest possibility in God. It seems to declare that man's love for man makes him the more godlike, and brings him nearer God.

"A man may o'ertake
God's own speed in the one way of love."

The lyric poems of the two poets are hard to compare. Tennyson's have a musical swing, and a beauty of form and thought which is nowhere surpassed. Yet Browning's lyrics, through Browning's own in style and theme are in every way equally praiseworthy.

It is interesting to observe the two in their dramatic works. Tennyson's whole life was marked by growth, and in his last period, in which he wrote the dramas, he was still growing. Therefore his dramas are his deepest and most finished products. But Browning had reached the pinnacle of his art in his dramatic monologues. Their form was best suited to his style because it was so utterly impossible for him to change his style with every character, and this the ideal dramatist must do.

Perhaps the least great of Tennyson's dramas is "The Falcon." It is pretty but the plot is shallow, too shallow, almost, to use for a drama. Yet each character is distinct, and Tennyson has succeeded in creating a style for each character. The whole is well wrought out, and pleasing, with a mild dramatic interest.

The most stageable of Browning's dramas, "The Blot on the Scutcheon" is somewhat melodramatic in plot, but this is saved by the wonderful poetic treatment. The style, however, is Browning's throughout, and does not change with the characters.

The dramas of both poets are more easily read than acted, with few exceptions. Yet there is a real stage charm, and true literary greatness in the dramatic works of each.

And so, throughout their works both are praiseworthy. We could not spare either of them, if we wish the whole manhood field, social as well as individual, before us. To complete the perfect view both men are necessary. Each of them had his own work, ideals and philosophy. Each lived his life nobly, and according to the principles which he held. Let us then, instead of haggling over which is the greater, always a disputable question, rather rejoice that we are fortunate enough to benefit by the teachings of both.

Florence K. Wilson, '11.

JAPANESE LULLABY.

I.

Little brown laddie with slanting eyes—
Dear little son of Japan
Your mother just loves you with all of her heart—
As only a Jap mother can.

II

Your little brown head is cuddled up close—
So close in the curve of my arm,
And I look in your eyes and dream my dreams,
And pray for your safety from harm.

III

Yet always, away from the dear home nest—
So soon do the birdlings fly,
And some day, you'll enter this great wide world
As the son of a Samurai.

IV

'Tis a name to be proud of, my little son,
The noblest in all Japan—
And your ancestors bore is without a stain—
As only the heroes can.

V

Thy father's sword is waiting for thee,
A hero's sword for a hero's son,
And thy father's glory will come to thee
When thy soldier's fame is won.

VI

Sleep on little laddie with slanting eyes,
Dreams sweet—little son of Japan.
The soul of a hero looks out from your eyes,
And I love you as only a Jap mother can.

Frances A. Cameron, '11.

SKETCHES

THE HURDY-GURDY.

When Molly Harding had sent for Cousin Veronica, a distant relative of her husband's, recently left penniless, she had expected that the old lady would be excellent company for Grandma Miller. Unfortunately Grandma Miller took an instant and violent dislike to Cousin Veronica who promptly returned the sentiment. All Molly's efforts to bring the two into harmony were unavailing. If one old lady expressed a liking for anything from knitting to baked beans, the other at once showed her scorn for the thing in question. They failed to be reconciled even by the children for Cousin Veronica "favored" Betty and Grandma saw only Teddy. Molly had almost despaired when an unforeseen incident righted matters.

One day an unusual sound broke the country quiet, the tinkle of a hurdy-gurdy playing, "Dear, dear, what can the matter be?" Hurdy-gurdies were rare. Two small, eager figures rushed out to the road. Two other figures met at the door, each with a nickel in hand. Evasion was impossible; they were caught in a mutual enthusiasm.

"'Tain't the piano-thing; it's the music," Cousin Veronica explained, stiffly. "We sang it in singing school."

Grandma was recalling things too, and the words slipped out before she knew, "So did we. O, ain't it pretty!"

Sometime later Molly, passing Grandma Miller's room, stopped in amazement. There at the window sat two old ladies, rocking and knitting, and contentedly singing, though with frequent breaks, "Swing Low, Sweet Chariot."

The hurdy-gurdy had done it.

L. Mc. H., '13.

THE CHIMES.

Softly and sweetly the chimes rang out over the city playing the old familiar hymns, and as they played their music did not pass unheeded, but many people heard and stopped to listen. The hurrying business man as he passed along the street after a hard day's worries, glanced up as if in search of the sweet sound and then hastened on, refreshed and rested by what he had heard, and with a few precious strains still ringing in his ears. The children playing in the twilight stopped their games to listen and their boisterous shouts were hushed for the time. The clergyman in his study preparing for the service to which the bells were inviting his people, felt uplifted and inspired and thanked God for the power of music. Down in the poorer quarters where good music and higher things were almost unknown, the weary, crowded foreigners instinctively held their breath and wondered what this new feeling meant. Wherever there was a sick person, tired and discouraged, help to relieve the pain and new courage to bear it seemed somehow to come with every note. And so the melodious sounds penetrated into many a corner, to all classes and kinds of people, and nowhere did they fail to carry something good, something helpful wherever help was needed.

Elizabeth McCague, '13.

A RAINY DAY.

What a horrible day it was, she thought dismally. It had rained for the last week, and she didn't suppose it would ever stop. She heard the people downstairs laughing and joking, and wondered how anyone could be cheerful, in the present weather. She didn't see why Jack Newall hadn't asked her to go to the theater with the rest of the crowd anyway. That nasty Ethel Bray had said he was going to ask Dorothy. She didn't see what there was in Dorothy to like so well—of course, she had pretty hair, big brown eyes, and all the rest of it, but then—and she looked in a mirror reflectively. She had always liked Dorothy, but she did think she was getting a little—yes, just a little—conceited. There, it was raining harder. What a good thing it was she didn't have to go out that evening. She was certainly thankful Jack hadn't asked her to go to the theater. Two tears splashed down on the window pane—probably because she was so very thankful that he hadn't asked her. Just at this point the telephone rang. She went slowly down to answer it, but in five minutes was back, smiles predominating. "He said," she was saying to herself, "that he thought until just this minute that he would have to work this evening. He's coming around in their machine, so I can wear my good clothes even if it is raining. It looks real nice out, though. The rain makes everything look so pretty and green, and the flowers look so fresh. He said he would come early, so we could have a little ride first," she went on, singing and laughing between times, "and—yes—I'll wear my very prettiest white dress."

Alice Stoelzing,' 13.

After a year's experience in college we feel so well prepared to give advice on things in general, that when we meet a little Freshman looking as green, as though she had come fresh from the Emerald Isle, we feel like cornering her and giving her some worldly wisdom like that of old Polonius in Hamlet.

Dull not the palm with idle entertaining,
On those dark restful hours when lights are out;
But if the presidency of thy class looks good,
Stint not to show thy new-hatched friends thy love.

Costly thy habit as thy purse can buy,
But put not all thy glad rags on i' the first week,
Else then thou wilt not have the wherewithall
T' outshine the rest on some great show occasion.

This above all, to thine own self be true,
And do thy lessons as the days go by;
Write up thy themes and hand them in on time,
Think not that exam week will never come.
I tell thee that it will and thou shalt flunk,
Except thou do thy work from day to day.

Marguerite Lambie.

AN INCIDENT.

It was a beautiful clear, moonlight night. All was silent except for the incessant barking of the St. Bernard. He would not be quiet; it was plain that he wanted something and wanted that something very much. To that conclusion we came, for it was the only logical one. He could not have been barking at a person, for there was not a soul within sight or hearing. We tested his hunger, his thirst, but could not appeal to the animal within him. His barking continued and was by this time annoying for the hour was late. Deciding that we would see the matter to the end, two of us went out to the back porch to watch the manoeuverings of the dog. He barked incessantly for a few minutes, looked at us in his dumb appealing manner, then made several weak attempts at jumping high in the air—his head turned skyward. Ah! we had solved the mystery. The poor beast was barking at the moon! After that we had a greater respect for Nero, for he taught us a lesson. We learned that dogs too have aspirations, and it is not only humanity that cries for the moon.

L. K., '13.

FROM A FRESHMAN'S DIARY.

May 26.

Well, I refuse to bother my head any more about that horrid, old comet. I was on duty, as usual, last night but I didn't see it, no, nor the least sign of it. The heavens clouded up so thickly you couldn't see any sky at all—much less a star. I sat down at the end of the board walk and scanned the heavens for an hour and a half. Finally the clouds seemed to loosen up and one or two stars appeared. All at once I caught a glimpse of a big bright star which had a peculiar twinkle to it and I felt sure it was the comet, for it was in the southwest and that's where it was to be. I rushed to the house to spread the news. Jane nearly fell down the stairs trying to get out before it absented itself again. About nine of the girls believed me and rejoiced with me, but the rest—sarcastic creatures—laughed and jeered and said we didn't know a star when we saw it, that the comet was farther north, for Miss Brady had seen it the night before. Betty's sister phoned from Allegheny and said that they couldn't help but see it over there. She said that the tail was plainly seen and looked to be a yard long. But we didn't see any tail attached to our star, so we decided it was not the comet. Alas! my dreams vanished, my heart crushed, and all for the sake of an old star with a tail.

Helen Blair, '13.

THE SOROSIS

Published Monthly by the Students of

Pennsylvania College for Women.

Ethel Tassey, '10 .... Editor-in-Chief
Elma McKibben, 10 .... Business Manager
Minerva Hamilton, '11 .... Literary Editor
Elvira Estep, '12 .... College Notes
Calla Stahlman, '12 .... Personals
Lillian McHenry, '13 .... Exchanges
Gertrude Wayne, '11 .... Assistant Business Manager

Subscriptions to the Sorosis 75 cents per year. Single copies 10c
Address all business communications to the Business Manager.
Entered in the Postoffice at Pittsburg, Pa., as second-class matter

With the June number of the Sorosis the 1909-1910 staff of editors step aside to make way for the new staff of 1910-1911 As we sever our active connections with the Sorosis we do not feel that the separation is final. The Alumnae columns are still open to us and we know from experience how welcome we shall be to them.

Needless to say the past year has not been perfect nor has it resulted in complete fulfillment of our desires; still in spite of drawbacks and disappointments we feel that on the whole it has been a very successful year. At least we have done our best and what more would be possible? From time to time we have attempted slight changes, especially in the appearance of the paper, which we flatter ourselves were real improvements. We also conducted a Short Story Contest, carrying out the plans of a former editor, Miss Lillia A. Greene, '07, who originated these contests and has furnished the prizes.

We wish to thank all those who have shown their interest in any way, by contributions or subscriptions and we would ask that you be as kind to the new Staff; join us in welcoming them and in wishing them all success in the year to come.

ALUMNAE NOTES

Miss Edna McKee was among the guests who attended the tea given in honor of the Seniors byMiss Brownson and Mrs. Armstrong.

Miss Carla Jarecki, '09 is visiting the College during Commencement week.

The engagement of Miss Lelia Estep, '09 to Mr. Jamison has been announced.

Decade Club II were to have welcomed the Seniors into membership at a picnic to have been held at the home of Mrs. Phillips of Carrick, but the meeting has been indefinitely postponed.

Mrs. Decker recently presented the College with a number of volumes for the library.

COLLEGE NOTES.

College Commencement will be held on the evening of June thirteenth in the College Chapel. The procession will include the graduating class, the board of trustees, the student body, and the alumnae. The speaker for the evening will be the Rev. Washington Gladden, D.D., LL.D., of Columbus. Ohio.

Class Day will be on Saturday, eleventh of June, when the Senior will present "The Romancers."

Plans are being made for a dance to be given the night after Commencement in honor of the Seniors. It will be very informal, since the house will be closed by that time.

Dr. and Mrs. Lindsay entertained the Seniors and Faculty at luncheon at the University Club, Saturday, May twenty-eighth. It was a most delightful affair, and all praised it highly.

The Seniors were guests of the Sophomore Class at luncheon in the "Green Room" at McCreery's Saturday afternoon, June fourth.

Four of the members of the Social Service Class made very interesting little speeches last Wednesday about the places they have visited during the year, and gave us a very good idea of the work that is being done along this line.

The members of Misses Brownson and Brownlee's table gave a party in honor of Misses Blakeslee and Christine Cameron, Thursday evening, June second; in honor of Miss Elizabeth McCague, Thursday, May twenty-sixth; and of Miss Stahlmann, Monday evening, May sixteenth.

Dr. Lindsay addressed the Y. W. C. A. Tuesday evening, May thirty-first. This was the last meeting of the Association for the year. Officers were elected May seventeenth for next year. They are as follows: President, Lillian McHenry; Vice President, Noeline Hickson; Secretary, Esther O'Neil; Treasurer, Helen Blair.

Mrs. Armstrong and Miss Brownson were hostesses at a tea in honor of the Seniors, Wednesday afternoon, June first, in South Hall. The affair was most charming.

Saturday, May twenty-first witnessed the celebration of the annual May Festival on the campus. A change was made in the character of the program. The College represented the old English spirit of May-Day, the crowning of the Queen a transition, and Dilworth Hall represented the modern spirit of May-Day. Miss Mabel Crowe who was crowned Queen of the May was attended by Misses Belle McClymonds, Florence Wilson, Martha Sands, Esther O'Neil and Jeannette Roenigh.

Saturday evening, May twenty-first, a "Surprise Party" was given, which turned out to be a Lantern Party. To the beat of two drums, and under the leadership of Miss Kathan, a long procession marched from Berry Hall to the gymnasium, where each was presented with a Japanese lantern. Thence the procession wended its way in and out over Woodland Road and the campus, ending with an impromptu drill on the campus, a march through Berry Hall.

MUSIC NOTES.

On the afternoon of May twenty-fourth, at four thirty o'clock, Miss Olive Woodburn, Miss Ruth Aiken, Miss Eunice Graham, Miss Margaret Greene, Miss Margaret Bonsall and Miss Helen Duff gave a musical recital, in the drawing rooms. The weather was quite disagreeable, but a large audience was present, notwithstanding.

The Annual Concert by the advanced students in music was given Friday evening, May twenty-seventh, at eight fifteen o'clock. Those appearing on the program were Misses Beech, Stahlmann, Horst, Detchon, Wehling, Leedom, pianists, and Misses Sands, Kerr, Bickel and Donovan, vocalists. The College Glee Club contributed two numbers. An enthusiastic and appreciative audience was in attendance.

The last of a series of five musical recitals was given Thursday afternoon at four o'clock in the Drawing Rooms. Those taking part on the program were Miss Susie Homer, pianist; and Misses Lucille Shurmer and Helen Kerr, sopranos. These recitals have been most interesting, since the programs have included such a large number of old and modern writers, and American as well as foreign composers.

OMEGA NOTES.

The last meeting of the Omega Society for the year was held at the home of Mr. Putman. The novels of Mrs. Humphry Ward were discussed. Miss Hamilton, '11, read a sketch of the life of Mrs. Ward; Miss Hardy, '12, read a paper on "Robert Elsmere" and "The Testing of Diana Mallory" was discussed by Miss Medley, '11. After the program Mrs. Putnam served tea.

Miss Beard, '09, and Miss Cohen, '09, former members of the society, were present.

PERSONALS.

Miss Marie Shinn and her mother of Carnegie attended the musical recital, the afternoon of May seventeenth, and visited in South Hall.

Miss Ionia Smith visited the Misses Marshall of Rochester, Pa., over Decoration Day.

Miss Calla Stahlmann spent Decoration Day with Miss Jane Linderman of Herron Hill.

A great deal of interest is being taken in the German company which will present several German plays at the Alvin theater next week. Several of the German classes will be represented at the production of "Minna von Barnhelm" on Wednesday.

Tuesday afternoon, May thirty-first, Mrs. Early delightfully entertained the Seniors and "English XVII" at her home on Murray Hill. The color scheme was carried out in lavendar and white and the guests received favors of lavendar sweet-peas.

Mrs. Lindsay has returned home from the South, but is spending a few weeks at Markleton Sanitarium.

Miss Lillian Lloyd, of St. Louis, expects to return to P. C. W., after a year spent in a local institution.

Miss Skilton and Miss Lovejoy entertained the Smith College Club at tea in South Hall, Wednesday, May 25th.

The College tennis tournament was won by Miss Beulah Pierce, '12. On June seventh the finals were held with Dilworth Hall and Miss Noeline Hickson, D. H. now holds the cup.

We are all glad to learn that Madame de Valley is recovering from her recent illness and will soon be with us again.

John Brownlee of W. and J., '11, visited Miss Janet Brownlee, Thursday evening, May twenty-sixth.

Mrs. J. C. Stahlmann, Mr. and Mrs. A. E. Young and Mrs. J. S. Whitworth of Vandergrift were guests in South Hall, May twentieth and twenty-first, and attended the May Day Fête.

Miss Elsie Weihe visited her home in Connellsville, Pa., May twenty-seventh to thirtieth.

Mrs. Coolidge has been suffering from a severe attach of tonsilitis.

Miss Ruth Peck and her mother, stopped at the College en route from Warren, Pa. to their home in Concordia, Kansas. We hope to have Miss Peck with us again next year.

Misses Jean and Lillian Marshall of Rochester, Pa., visited Ionia Smith on May Day, May twenty-first.

EXCHANGES.

The following verses appeared in the "Gownsman," the Oxford publication, shortly before Roosevelt's visit to the university:

The lion and the unicorn will scatter for their lives,
When the mighty big game hunter from America arrives;
But his progress in the jungle is as nothing to his fame
In copybook with Sunday chapel missionary game.

Oh, we're ready for you Teddy, our sins are all reviewed,
We've put away our novels and our statues in the nude,
We've read your precious homilies and hope to hear some more,
At the coming visitation of the moral Theodore.

Senior—"When I graduate I will step into a position at twenty thousand dollars per."

Sophomore—"Per what?"

Freshman—"Per-haps."—Ex.

Applied Mathematics.

"My daughter," and his voice was stern,
"You must set this matter right;
What time did the Sophomore leave,
Who sent his card last night?"
"His work was pressing, father dear
And his love for it was great;
He took his leave and went away
Before a quarter of eight."
Then a twinkle came to her bright blue eye,
And her dimple deeper grew,
"'Tis surely no sin to tell him that,
For a quarter of eight is—two."—Ex.

"When I arose to speak," related a martyred statesman, "some one hurled a base, cowardly egg at me, and it struck me in the chest."

"And what kind of an egg might that be?" asked a fresh young man.

"A base, cowardly egg," explained the statesman, "is one that hits you and then runs."—Ex.

Don't be what yo' ain't
Ef yo' ain't what yo' is;
Ef yo' isn't what yo' am not,
Den yo' am not what yo' is!—Ex.

Student—Want my hair cut.
Barber—Any special way?
Student—Yes, off.—Ex.

CPSIA information can be obtained
at www.ICGtesting.com
Printed in the USA
BVHW071736121218
535437BV00032B/2005/P